ISLAND OF THE MINOTAUR

GREEK MYTHS OF ANCIENT CRETE

To my queen, Lisa — S.O.

To Annie - wife, muse, confidante, Ariadne - and occasionally beloved antagonist. Thanks for the grit and the grace—B.D.

First American edition published in 2004 by
CROCODILE BOOKS
An imprint of Interlink Publishing Group Inc.
46 Crosby Street, Northampton, Massachusetts 01060
www.interlinkbooks.com

Published in Great Britain and Canada by Tradewind Books Limited

Text copyright © 2004 by Sheldon Oberman
Illustrations copyright © 2004 by Blair Drawson

Library of Congress Cataloging-in-Publication Data available

ISBN 1-56656-531-6

This book was typeset in Legacy Sans and Lithos.

Color separations by ScanLab, Vancouver

Technical and pre-press assistance by Westpoint Graphics, Vancouver

Printed and bound in Korea
10 9 8 7 6 5 4 3 2 1

Book and jacket design by Elisa Gutiérrez

Chapter graphics by Elisa Gutiérrez

Additional layout by Jacqueline Wang

ISLAND OF
THE MINOTAUR

GREEK MYTHS OF ANCIENT CRETE

Sheldon Oberman  Illustrated by Blair Drawson

Crocodile Books, USA

An imprint of Interlink Publishing Group, Inc.

NEW YORK • NORTHAMPTON

My thanks to Professor Robert Gold, who introduced me to ancient Crete some thirty years ago and has more recently—along with Professors Jane Cahill and Mark Golden—helped me stay true to both the details and the spirit of these myths. And lastly, to my daughter, Mira, who helped me edit the final stages of this book.

— Sheldon Oberman

Many thanks to Mike Katz for his patience, endurance and vision. And to Elisa Gutiérrez for her skill in making my own work look good.

— Blaire Drawson

The publisher wishes to thank Dr. Robert Cousland, Associate Professor of Religious Studies at the University of British Columbia, for his help.

The publisher also wishes to thank the young readers of the Novel Knickers Book Club for their help, and Aniko Kiss for her photographic work on an earlier version of this book.

INTRODUCTION

Here are the mythic tales of the Minoan Civilization woven into a continuous story of heroic quests, clever tricks, puzzles and disguises. Meet Theseus and Ariadne, Jason and Medea, Daedalus and Icarus, King Minos and Hercules. Meet the gods Rhea, Cronos, Zeus and Poseidon and the strange creatures of a distant world—the Ash Tree Spirits, Pan the goat boy, Talus the Bronze Giant, the Great White Bull and the monstrous Minotaur. ✷ Crete, an island in the Mediterranean, was the home of the great but mysterious people we now call the Minoans. We don't know what they called themselves, but we do know that their civilization lasted almost 1,500 years (3,000 BC to 1,450 BC). We know they had fast and powerful ships, which they used to guard their shores and to explore the Mediterranean and beyond. They built ninety beautiful towns and cities, not one of them fortified by walls. The Minoans had sunlit palaces filled with works of art where they feasted and watched thrilling rituals that involved somersaulting over bulls. We can only guess about the mysteries, which they kept hidden in the chambers beneath their palaces and in the deep caves of their mountains. ✷ Their world was utterly lost. We only know about them through the myths of the ancient Greeks, who were ruled by the Minoans until they broke free and became a great power themselves. One of the most famous tales the Greeks told was the history of their struggle with the Minoans, which became the myth of Theseus and the Minotaur. ✷ Myths have a wonderful way of simplifying and dramatizing complicated events. The thousands of years it took for Crete to develop a civilization were turned into a tale of three generations of gods—the primitive god, Uranos; then his cruel son, Cronos; and finally, the civilized Zeus. The army of Bronze Age warriors that defended Crete's shores became Talus, the Bronze Giant. Crete's many inventors and engineers became a single person, Daedalus. Two thousand years later, Sir Arthur Evans, the archaeologist and adventurer, became part of the great story when he discovered the remains of the lost civilization and named it Minoa. ✷ Minoa's most dramatic event was the volcanic eruption that destroyed it. This catastrophe became one of the world's most famous myths. It occurred on a nearby Minoan island called Kalliste, which was later called Thera. It was one of the largest eruptions of the past 100,000 years, with the power of 150 hydrogen bombs and an explosion that could be heard a continent away. Earthquakes, tidal waves and volcanic ash followed the blast. Kalliste was nearly obliterated. Much of it collapsed into the sea, leaving behind only a volcanic shell. The island of Crete was devastated and the civilization of the Minoans was destroyed. Countless works of wonder and beauty were lost forever. ✷ Even the story of the disaster was nearly lost. Centuries later, Plato, an ancient Greek philosopher, repeated a tale he had heard about an island civilization that was suddenly destroyed. He called the island Atlantis. The story came to Plato from Egypt. When we sort out the Egyptian dates and details, we find that Atlantis was destroyed at the same time, in the same way and very likely in the same location as Kalliste. People assumed that the story was nothing more than a fantasy, but it seems the myth may have been true. ✷ We will never know for certain, but we do know this: Kalliste was as wonderful as any Atlantis. Its destruction brought to an end a great and mysterious civilization. King Minos' palace on Crete was the size of Buckingham Palace. Typical houses excavated on Kalliste were highly sophisticated with advanced plumbing and astonishing art. The splendid cities are gone, the amazing inventions and swift ships are lost. Even the language has disappeared. But the stories live on. Here they are, carefully retold from the earliest sources, fresh and full of wonders. ✷

CONTENTS

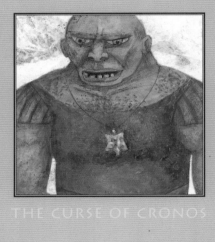

THE CURSE OF CRONOS

THE CURSE OF CRONOS

A CRIME OF BLOOD

"I WILL PROTECT YOU FROM CRONOS," the Goddess Rhea whispered to her unborn baby. She would not let him take this baby as he had taken all her others.

Cronos was the Angry God who ruled from a stormy sky. He had seized power from his father, Uranos, the first god to rule the world. Hungry for power, Cronos attacked Uranos with a curved stone knife as he lay sleeping in his starry bed. The Old God howled in pain and rage, for though Uranos was immortal and could not die, he could suffer and lose his power. As Uranos felt his great strength drain away, he called a curse upon his son:

You will fall as I have fallen.
Your own child will defeat you.

Three drops of the Old God's blood fell to the earth below and sank into the soil. The blood boiled and hissed until the earth began to swell. Out burst three ghastly creatures with writhing snakes for hair. They were the Furies, demons of Guilt, Shame and Terror. They were born to follow Cronos wherever he went and to haunt him with his father's words:

You will fall as your father fell.
Your own child will defeat you.

Three more drops of blood fell from the sky like small red seeds. Two drops grew into ash trees. The third drop grew into a tree of long twisted horns. When night came, the three trees transformed into strange and gentle creatures. Two became female spirits of the trees, and the third became a mother goat with twisted horns. They silently departed, heading for the Forest of Dicte on the island of Crete. They would wait there for a special child to be born who would someday defeat Cronos.

"Your own child will defeat you!" Uranos kept shouting until Cronos could stand it no longer.

He raised Uranos above his head and threw him out of the sky. The Old God fell screaming into the Pit of Tartarus, which lay in the darkest depths of the Deep

9

Gorge of the Earth. Still furious, Cronos hunted down the fiercely loyal monster children of Uranos—first the Hundred-Handed Giants and then the vengeful Cyclopes. Cronos conquered each and every one of them. Then he flung them one after another into the Pit, which was too deep to escape, too dark for any light to ever reach.

Still, Cronos felt danger all around him. He built a fortress out of storm clouds on Mount Othrys. He summoned his brothers, the Titans, and he had them swear that they would serve him as loyal warriors. Then, with no one to oppose him, he seized the lovely goddess Rhea and he forced her to be his wife.

"Now I control all things," Cronos boasted. But he could not control his fear. Not when the Furies whispered:

> You will fall as your father fell
> Your own child will defeat you.

Cronos blocked his ears with his huge stony fists and roared, "Never! Never!"

. . . .

THE BIRTH CAVE

Rhea had given birth five times. Cronos had always been watching and waiting, determined to stop her children from growing up to threaten him.

Each time, his voice thundered from the sky, "Give me the child!"

Each time, Rhea tried desperately to save it. Each time, she failed.

When Rhea hid inside the earth, Cronos bombarded her with bolts of lightning. He blasted through the rock and soil, and his thunder shook her senseless. She awoke to find that her child was gone.

When Rhea ran into the sea, Cronos swirled the water into whirlpools that pulled the child from her arms. When Rhea flew into the sky, Cronos hunted her with wind and cloud. The clouds blinded her. The winds tore the child away.

Rhea could not hide even in the Underworld, which was crowded with the spirits of the dead and the dreams of the sleeping. Cronos commanded all the dead and dreaming to do his will. Ghosts and nightmares swarmed around her, filling her with such terror that she lost her grip on the child. Rhea could do nothing but watch helplessly as the child hovered just beyond her reach, then disappeared.

Each time Cronos seized a child, he transformed into a towering black cloud. His mouth became a whirling funnel that swallowed the infant whole. The children were immortal, so Cronos could not destroy them. But he could keep them trapped and helpless. He swallowed all of Rhea's five children and held them in the prison of his stormy body.

"Nothing can escape me," Cronos said. "I know about all things on the earth and in the sea, the sky and the world below. I control all things."

Rhea loved all things. She had to try to save her sixth child, the one who was about to be born. As Rhea flew over Mount Dicte on the island of Crete, she heard loving voices singing to her from below.

> *Come down to us.*
> *Be safe with us.*
> *We wait.*
> *We wait for you.*

The gentle beauty of the song drew Rhea down from the sky. She found the three singers waiting for her in front of a mountain cave. They were the Kind Ones: Adrasteia and Io, Spirits of the Ash Trees, and the Great Mother Goat, Amalthea.

They gazed into her eyes and sang:

> *We three were born from blood and earth,*
> *To hide, protect the new god's birth.*

As they turned and walked into the cave, Rhea followed. They led her from cavern to cavern through groves of stalagmites and stalactites, until finally they came to the largest cavern of all. They stood aside as Rhea entered and saw a full-grown, living ash tree glowing in the darkness. Its strongest branch held a cradle made of gold.

"How can you protect my baby?" Rhea asked them. "Cronos knows about all things on the earth and in the sea, the sky and the world below."

The Kind Ones answered softly, "This cradle is not on the earth, nor in the sea, the sky, nor the world below. It hangs upon our ash tree sister, whose branches sway without a wind, whose leaves can sigh and sing and hide your child. Even from the eyes of Cronos."

Rhea began to cry, not with sorrow, but with relief. Her tears flowed down over her cheeks and seemed to wash away all her fears. She nodded to the Kind Ones and said, "I shall have my baby here."

. . . .

12

THE SHINING ONE

Rhea felt her baby coming. She knelt and clutched the earth, calling out, "Mother Gaea, Goddess of the Earth, if you love me then love my child! Send me my nine brothers, the Curetes."

Something rumbled beneath her and she felt the ground becoming warm and soft. Nine warriors rose out of the earth, each one armed with a bronze sword and shield.

"Brothers, I need your help," she told them. "My child is coming. Cronos, the Angry God, must not know or he will hunt me down and swallow the child. Guard the cave from any creature who serves him."

That very night the baby was born, glowing so brightly that it lit the cave.

Rhea said, "I shall call him Zeus, which means the Shining One."

She placed Zeus in the golden cradle and rocked him till he fell asleep.

"Now, I must go to the Fortress of Storms where Cronos stands and watches," she said. "My baby will never be truly safe unless I face Cronos."

"You cannot fight the Angry God," her brothers answered.

"No," she said, "but perhaps I can trick him."

And she left.

· · · · · · · · · ·

NOTHING BUT A STONE

Baby Zeus woke up crying hot tears for his mother. The Ash Tree Spirits sang. The goat, Amalthea, rocked his cradle. But Zeus cried even louder, until the whole cave shook.

"These are the cries of a god," said the Tree Spirits. "Cronos will hear and come for the child."

Rhea's nine brothers struck their swords upon their shields. They stamped their feet and sang high and wild words, desperately trying to drown out the baby's cries.

Far away in his stormy fortress, Cronos was listening. At that moment, Rhea appeared before him.

"I hear your brothers shouting," Cronos said. "Why are they in such a frenzy?"

Rhea answered softly. "You are hearing their song of defeat. They are wailing out their grief, because they cannot stop you from taking my baby."

Cronos stared at the bundle in her arms. He saw the sheets and blankets, but he did not see what they held. It was a smooth stone, the size and shape of a baby.

"Give the child to me," Cronos demanded.

"No!" Rhea answered. "Only the lowest beast would swallow its young."

Then she flew away, clutching the bundle in her arms.

Cronos was furious.

"Good," she whispered to herself. "Let him get even angrier."

Cronos' thunder crashed around her. His lightning burned her, but she kept flying. She swooped and turned, again and again, constantly avoiding being caught yet never trying to get away. She wanted to drive Cronos into a fury, to make him so blind with rage that he would swallow the stone without stopping to see or feel it.

Rhea saw the lightning flash just before it struck her. She crashed into a dusty field. When she looked up from the dirt, she saw Cronos high above her. He was growing as huge and wide as the sky itself. His winds swirled all around her and tore the ragged bundle from her arms. She watched the bundle rise, spiralling up toward him.

Rhea clutched the earth and prayed again to her mother, "Gaea, Goddess of the Earth, do not let the cloth unravel. Do not let Cronos see that it holds nothing but a stone."

The bundle disappeared into the storm cloud. There was a last burst of thunder followed by silence. The Angry God had swallowed it.

Rhea lay bruised and bleeding. She whispered to the earth, "My baby is safe. He will grow, and one day he will set all my other children free."

The cloud rumbled and moved on across the sky, heading to Cronos' Fortress of Storms on Mount Othrys. Rhea heard him laughing like distant thunder.

"I defeated her," he boasted.

"We will see who is defeated," she whispered.

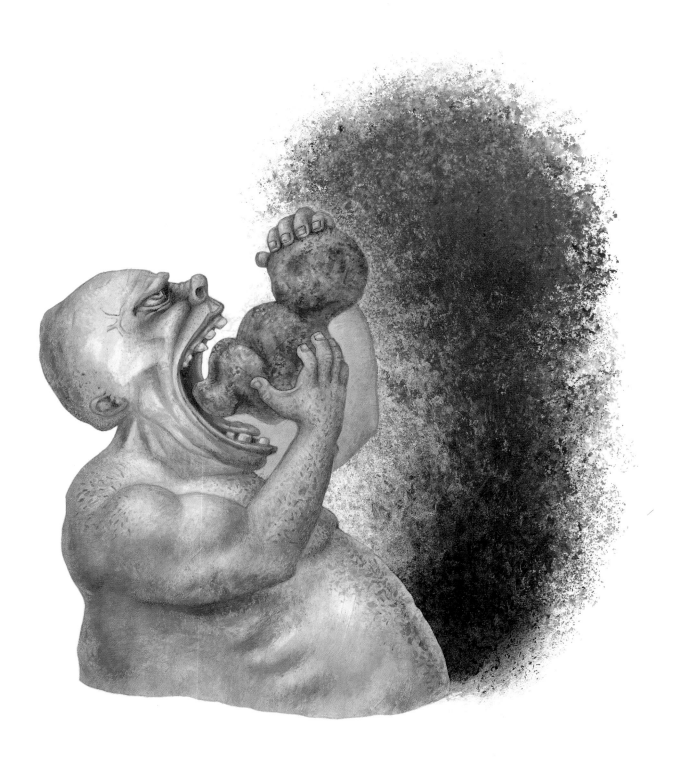

ZEUS AND THE OLYMPIANS

ZEUS AND THE OLYMPIANS

OUT OF A DARKENING SKY

THE KIND ONES KEPT ZEUS, THE IMMORTAL BABY, hidden in their secret cave on Crete. Cronos, the Angry God, thought that he had swallowed Zeus. He was sure that he had Zeus trapped inside him, along with all of Rhea's other children. Zeus' mother, Rhea, stayed far away from the cave. She did not want Cronos to grow suspicious and discover where Zeus really was.

The Tree Spirits fed Baby Zeus ambrosia, the food of the gods. They directed the bees to feed him honey. Amalthea, the Great Mother Goat, fed him her own milk.

Zeus grew quickly. Soon milk, honey and ambrosia were not enough. Amalthea, the Great Mother Goat, lowered her head and let Zeus pull her horn. The spiral horn broke off. Out spilled fruits, cheeses, nuts and berries. Zeus laughed and ate it all. Yet there was always more food in the horn, whatever he desired. This was the gift of Amalthea. It was called Cornucopia, the Horn of Plenty.

Zeus soon grew big enough to leave the cave. He spent his childhood on the slopes of Mount Ida, where shepherds still bring their sheep to graze. Rhea's brothers tried to guard him, but he was faster than all of them. He grew taller and stronger, more handsome and more clever. Yet, he did not know he was a god.

Zeus played with his only friend, Pan, the son of the Great Mother Goat. Pan was half human, half goat. Together, Zeus and Pan wrestled and swam, climbed and raced. One day, they were throwing spears at a lone oak tree, when a storm swept over the mountain. Suddenly, out of the darkening sky, a bolt of lightning shot straight toward Pan.

"No!" Zeus shouted. Without thinking, he reached out and caught the bolt. He held it quivering in his hand. Yet, he was not hurt. Zeus and Pan stared in amazement. A smile spread across the young god's face.

"Watch this," Zeus said.

He threw the lightning bolt. It struck the oak tree, blasting it to bits. Zeus' mother, Rhea, watched and nodded to herself from a distant cloud.

"My son has learned he is a god," she said. "Now it is time for us to face Cronos."

. . . .

THE POTION OF RELEASE

Rhea had a plan. She went to her sister, Metis, who knew the secret weakness of every living thing. Metis knew that Cronos was afraid of losing control, so she made a powder to mix with his wine. She called it the Potion of Release.

Three days later, according to their plan, Zeus and Rhea entered Cronos' Fortress of Storms. Zeus was dressed as a servant. He kept his head bowed so Cronos would not see the immortal glow of his face or the fierce determination in his eyes.

"Great Cronos," said Rhea, "I have brought this young man to be your servant."

Cronos sneered at Zeus and commanded him, "Fill my cup, you beardless boy."

As Zeus filled the huge drinking cup, his hands began to shake.

Cronos snarled, "Stop trembling, coward, or you'll spill the wine."

He turned away from Zeus and stared at Rhea. "Why did you bring me such a weakling?"

Zeus was only pretending to be afraid. As he poured the wine, his trembling hand shook the invisible powder into the wine.

As Cronos raged at Rhea, the red wine in the cup bubbled and turned a sickly green, then turned back to red again. Cronos saw nothing and suspected nothing. He seized the cup and drank the wine the way he drank everything—draining the cup without tasting, smelling or thinking. A moment later he gasped. Then he grew pale and dropped the cup, spilling the last few drops.

"Are you trembling with fear, Mighty Cronos?" Zeus taunted. "Is that why you spilled your wine?"

"Poison!" Cronos roared.

His body was racked with spasms. Fighting against the pain, he grew into a giant, bursting through the ceiling of his palace. He transformed into a massive dark cloud, spewing torrents of rain as he tried to purge the potion from his body.

"Poison!" he roared again as he rocked with thunder and lightning.

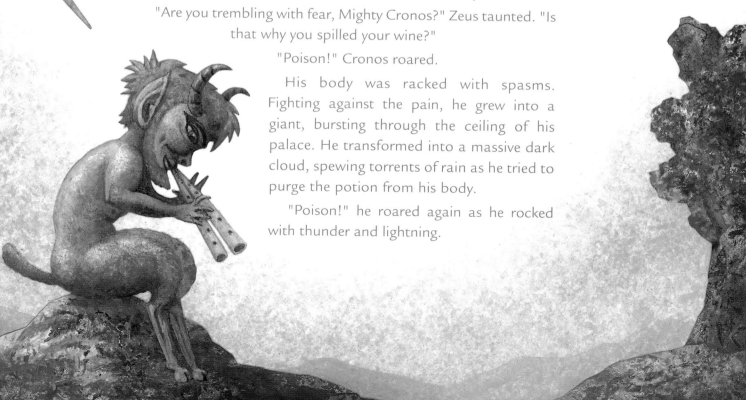

19

Suddenly, he heard shouts even louder than his own thunder. They came from within his own body—from the young gods he had swallowed. The first five children of Rhea—Hestia, Demeter, Hera, Hades and Poseidon—had grown tall and powerful and were breaking free from his belly.

Cronos had lost control. He panicked and fled the palace in confusion. That gave Zeus the time he needed. He led his brothers and sisters to another mountain and armed them for battle.

Zeus told them, "We cannot waste a moment. Cronos will recover from his fear. Then, he will be more dangerous than ever. We must build a fortress and prepare for war."

Zeus freed the Hundred-Handed Giants and the Cyclopes from their prison in the Pit of Tartarus. They joined him and brought three powerful weapons—thunderbolts for Zeus, the three-pronged trident spear for Poseidon and the helmet of invisibility for Hades.

Just as Zeus had predicted, Cronos regained his courage. He called upon his brothers, the Titans, who were the most deadly of all warriors, and led them in a terrible attack against the Young Immortals.

20

The War of the Gods had begun. It raged on for ten years, nearly destroying the entire world. Yet Cronos could not overcome Zeus and his brothers and sisters. He and his Titans fled, but the Young Immortals chased after them and found them, even though they hid in the most secret corners of the world. Cronos and his Titans were dragged to the Pit of Tartarus and cast into its depths. Cronos roared in horror as he tumbled through the darkness.

When he struck the very bottom of the Pit, he stood and howled in fury. But, just like his own father, he was helpless. The curse of Uranos had been fulfilled. Cronos had fallen as his father fell. His own son had defeated him.

After the War of the Gods ended, Zeus called a meeting of his brothers and sisters.

"Cronos tried to control everything," he said. "Instead, let us divide everything. Let each of us choose a different realm to rule."

Hera chose the earth and Poseidon chose the sea. Zeus took the sky, while Hades took the world below. Demeter ruled the fields of wheat and other growing things. Hestia became Goddess of the Home, so that all creatures could find places of shelter and comfort. Together, with Zeus as their leader, the gods built a palace on Mount Olympus. They called themselves the Olympians.

EUROPA'S WISH

EUROPA S WISH

BROTHERS OF THE SEA AND SKY

Zeus, God of the Sky, could transform into any shape he wished. One day, he became a cloud over Mount Olympus. He turned into rain and fell upon Hera, Goddess of the Earth. As he rained upon her, she laughed in delight and the earth blossomed with bright flowers. He transformed again, as the rain gathered into streams and then turned into a river that flowed into the sea.

Poseidon, God of the Sea, recognized his brother Zeus no matter what shape he took. Poseidon waited for him in his ocean chariot, which was pulled by dolphins. He waved his three-pronged spear and shouted, "Greetings, Brother Zeus, Cloud Gatherer, Master of the Thunderbolt! Why have you come to my wet world?"

"Greetings Brother Poseidon, Sea Stormer and Earth Shaker," Zeus answered, and he changed back into his true form as God of the Sky. "I have come for your help. Have you noticed the humans? Some of them are crossing your ocean in wooden vessels."

"They are weak and silly creatures," said Poseidon. "They look a bit like gods, but they don't live forever like we do. They die so quickly and easily."

"The ones from Phoenicia are good sailors," said Zeus. "I want them to teach their secrets of sailing to the people of Crete."

Poseidon laughed, "That's easy! Tell them to do it, or I will sink their ships with storms! I will smash their homes with earthquakes!"

"I have a better way," said Zeus. "Poseidon, you are the Herder of Bulls. I wish to take the shape of your finest bull. I am planning to play a trick that will get me exactly what I want."

"Of course, my brother," said Poseidon. "But why bother with a trick when you have the power of the entire sky?"

Zeus answered with a laugh, "Ha! Sometimes a clever trick can do more than all my bolts of lightning."

. . . .

23

A CLEVER TRICK

Zeus headed to Phoenicia on the eastern shore of the Mediterranean. He was searching for the princess of that land, the clever and skilful Europa. He found her on a beach gazing out to sea.

Her friends called to her from a nearby field, "Europa, come join us. We're picking flowers."

Europa shook her head and looked across the water, watching her father's ships, with their high wide sails and many long oars. Europa was bored and frustrated. She had learned so much, but she could do so little. She knew how to build and sail those long ships, but she was not allowed to. She gazed longingly at the docks across the bay. They were crowded with people who came from every land that touched the Mediterranean, and even from many lands that lay beyond. Europa had learned their languages, but she was not allowed to speak to them. She had learned about their lands, but she was not allowed to visit them.

She grumbled, "I am not allowed to do anything!"

Her father had told her that someday she would be Queen of Phoenicia, so she was too important to take risks. He made up countless rules to keep her safe. He even chose her friends and ordered them to stay with her, to watch her and to make sure that nothing happened to her.

"Nothing ever happens to me," she complained to the salty waves that lapped at her feet.

She picked up a flat stone from the beach and skipped it across the water. As it sank, Europa made a wish. "I wish that I could find some place with no rules but my own."

Zeus was standing on a far off hill, but he heard Europa speak her wish aloud. He smiled and murmured, "I will grant you your wish, Europa."

He strolled toward a herd of cattle that were grazing on the hillside. As he moved among the cows, he began to transform. His head grew horns. His face stretched long and his forehead stretched wide. His hands and feet hardened into hooves. He stamped the earth and became a bull.

A moment later Europa looked up. She saw the bull standing silently in the field. Her friends saw it, too.

"What a handsome animal," one of them said. "Its skin looks smooth as silk. Its horns are curved like crescent moons."

"It looks so gentle," Europa said.

24

They approached it cautiously. The bull hardly seemed to notice. They fed it grass and leaves. The bull licked their fingers. They draped garlands of flowers around its neck, and the bull nudged their hands for more.

Europa cooed, "It's just a big cuddly pet." She rubbed its broad smooth back, and the bull folded its legs and knelt upon the ground.

"Look at me!" a friend called out, as she climbed upon its back. The bull closed its eyes as if it were falling asleep.

"It's my turn," Europa sang out cheerfully.

She climbed upon the bull and whispered into its ear, "Poor thing, you are just like me. They make you look pretty. They feed you and fuss over you. But you can only do what you are told to do."

The bull opened its eyes. It rose with the dignity of a king and walked proudly across the field toward the sea.

"It's giving me a ride!" Europa laughed.

"You really should get off," one of her friends warned her.

Another pulled the bull's horn to make it stop. The bull snorted and began to trot. "Jump!" they called to Europa, but by then the bull was galloping over sharp rocks. "It's heading into the water!" they cried.

The bull did not leap into the surf. Instead, it charged over the surface of the sea as if the waves were solid ground.

Europa held on tightly, shouting, "Stop!"

But the bull kept rushing forward.

She called back to her friends, "Help me!"

But the bull had already taken her so far that she could not hear them answer. Her friends seemed to be shrinking into the distance. Then the land itself fell away, and there was only the wide sea all around her. Europa beat her fists against the bull's thick neck and yelled, "Where are you taking me?"

The beast answered with a human voice, "I have granted you your wish, Europa. You wished for a place with no rules. I am taking you to an island that no one has ever ruled."

"You monster!" she cried out. "The gods will punish you for this!"

The bull laughed and asked, "What gods would dare to punish Zeus?"

"Are you the mighty Zeus? What do you want with me?" she asked.

The bull did not answer and Europa was afraid to ask again. She held on tightly, as the bull galloped over the wine dark sea.

26

When they reached the island, Europa leapt off. She was about to run away, when the bull transformed into a handsome young man with a shining face. Europa dared a single glance. She saw Zeus gazing kindly at her, and she knew he would not hurt her.

He spoke to her softly, "Europa, this is the island of Crete where I was born and protected. I am grateful to its people. That is why I want you to teach them how to build great ships and how to sail the sea."

"Please," she begged. "I don't belong here. I want to go home."

"This is your new home," he said. "You wished for a place with no rules. No one here will ever tell you what to do."

Europa summoned her courage and looked into Zeus' shining eyes. She said, "You can make me stay here against my will. But, if you wish me to stay here willingly, then grant me the rest of my wish."

"What is the rest of your wish?" Zeus asked.

"I wished for a place with no rules but my own," she said.

Zeus narrowed his eyes and asked, "What do you mean?"

"Mighty Zeus, I am the daughter of a king. You were born to rule and so was I," said Europa. "Let me live upon this island by my own rules. Let me be its queen."

Zeus smiled. "You are both brave and clever," he said. "You will have your wish, and I will have mine."

So Europa became the Queen of Crete. She taught its people how to build and sail long narrow ships with high wide sails and many long oars. They became masters of the open sea and Crete became a powerful nation. ❦

THE BRONZE GIANT

THE BRONZE GIANT

THE THREE WISHES OF KING MINOS

Queen Europa taught the people of Crete how to build and sail great ships. They sailed freely throughout the Mediterranean, fishing, exploring new lands and trading with everyone they met. They became wealthy, but their wealth attracted pirates. The pirates attacked their ships at sea.

Soon the pirates grew bolder and more brutal. One day, the queen learned that the pirates had banded together. They were going to attack with a fleet of all their ships and overrun the island.

Queen Europa called her people to the palace and announced, "I have taught you how to build great ships and how to sail them, but I cannot teach you how to fight. My son, Minos, is now a man. Let him be king and defend the island."

She told Minos to sit on her alabaster throne, and she placed her crown of peacock feathers on his head.

"Now you rule Crete," she said.

Minos looked miserable. "I cannot do any good," he confessed. "I cannot fight the pirates. None of us can. We are a gentle and peace-loving people. Those pirates are cruel and bloodthirsty. How can we stand against them?"

"You must ask the god Zeus for help," his mother advised. "Approach Zeus with respect and he may grant you a wish. Wish carefully and you may get what you truly need."

The next morning, Minos led the people in a grand procession toward the birth cave of Zeus on Mount Dicte. They walked up the gentle slope and through the forest, singing songs of praise to Zeus. It was midnight when they reached the sacred cave.

Some of the people beat swords against bronze shields and sang wildly outside the cave, just as the Curetes, the Protectors of Zeus, had done long ago. Others swung wooden instruments, called *rhombi*, on long ropes to make the sound of Zeus' thunder. The rest lit torches and tossed them off the mountain to streak through the sky like Zeus' lightning. This pleased the God of the Sky, and his cave began to glow.

29

Minos entered but could not see the god. He called out, "Father Zeus, I am Minos, son of Europa. My mother has made me king. I have come for your help."

Zeus' voice rumbled through the cave, "What is your wish?"

Minos blurted out the first things that came to his mind. "Give us a wall that can protect our island. And an army clad in bronze that can last a thousand years. And a great warrior that no man can defeat!"

Zeus' laughter burst from the cave. The people outside fell to the ground in terror. "You have made three wishes, not one," said Zeus. "But since you have shown me great respect, I will give you all three wishes joined into one. You will find your wish granted at the edge of the sea."

"Thank you, mighty Zeus," Minos murmured. He hurried out of the cave and told the people, "Zeus granted us a wall, an army clad in bronze to last a thousand years and a warrior no man can defeat."

. . . .

THE WALL, THE ARMY AND THE WARRIOR

King Minos and his people hurried through the night and reached the sea, just as the sun was rising. The beach was empty. There was no wall, no army and no great warrior.

Minos fell to his knees, exhausted. "This is all my fault!" he moaned. "Zeus offered me a wish and I answered like a fool. I asked for too much, so he gave me nothing."

"Look!" yelled a boy staring out to sea. "Ships are coming. Maybe they are bringing all your wishes."

The ships were not bringing wishes. They were bringing pirates.

We have no chance against them, Minos thought to himself.

"Run! I will fight them as they land. That will give you time to escape."

"No," answered his people. "We must face them together."

Suddenly, a huge rock sailed over their heads and smashed the closest ship. Another rock flew through the air and struck the ship next to it. Minos turned to the forest behind him and saw a giant made of bronze towering above the trees. The giant lifted a boulder covered with grass and bushes. He hurled it at a third ship, and it shattered the ship's rudder so it could not steer. The ship turned helplessly in circles, as the giant marched through the waves toward it.

30

A dozen ships surrounded the giant. The pirates shot arrows and threw spears at him, but they bounced off his metal body.

The giant grasped one of the boats in his massive hands and began to crush it. The timbers creaked and groaned. Pirates cursed and hacked at him with their swords.

But it was no use. He cracked the ship in two. Then he raised both halves above his head and crashed them onto the nearest ship.

The rest of the fleet tried to escape. He seized the largest ship and, gripping it at each end, smashed it against the others until he sank them all.

Everything was still and silent except for the waves carrying wreckage to the beach. The people of Crete stared in confusion, not knowing whether to cheer or run away. The giant trudged back to shore and halted in front of Minos. His shadow covered the king like a dark cloud.

31

"What are you?" Minos asked.

The giant answered in a voice of grinding metal. "I am Talus, sent by Zeus."

"I did not wish for you," said Minos.

"I am your three wishes joined into one. I am the wall that can protect your island. I am the army clad in bronze that can last a thousand years. I am the warrior that no man can defeat."

Talus, the Bronze Giant, was the wish of Minos and the will of Zeus. He

marched along the shores of the island, guarding it day and night. He could sense an enemy ship long before it sailed into sight and was always ready. If he could not find rocks to throw, he would leap into the water and crush the enemy. At other times, he would build a bonfire and stand inside it, letting his bronze body glow bright red with heat. Then, as the enemy ship came close to the shore, he would attack and grip it in a fiery hug until the vessel burst into flames.

Crete was safe. The people did not need any other walls or warriors. They spent their time and wealth building beautiful cities and constructing grand ships that sailed the sea as freely as the clouds in Zeus' sky.

Every ninth year, which was called the Great Year, King Minos led his people to the sacred cave. He entered alone and thanked Zeus for the Bronze Giant. This pleased the god. The cave filled with light and Zeus gave the king wise answers to all his questions. ⚘

THE WILL OF ZEUS

THE WILL OF ZEUS

A DIFFERENT KING

WHEN KING MINOS GREW OLD, HIS SON BECAME THE KING OF CRETE. When that son grew old, his son took the throne. So it went for centuries. Each king grew old and a young king took his place. However, Talus, the Bronze Giant sent by Zeus, did not grow old. He kept pacing the shores of the island, always ready to defend it.

Then a new king took power who was different from the others. He was named Minos, like the first king, but he had no respect for anyone, not even for Zeus. When the Great Year came, he did not walk to the mountain cave, as all the other kings had done. He drove a golden chariot pulled by a proud black horse. The people beat their swords against their shields and sang. They made the roar of Zeus' thunder and the flash of Zeus' lightning. However, this King Minos only smirked, as though it were a joke. He sauntered into the cave, as though he expected Zeus to greet him like a beloved son. But the cave did not fill with light, as it had always done for all the other kings. And Zeus was not there to grant a wish or to offer wise advice.

Zeus was far away beneath the ocean. He was speaking to Poseidon, God of the Sea. "This new king does not respect me," Zeus said. "I gave his ancestors a great gift, but I will not let him keep it."

"Will you take it back?" asked Poseidon.

"No", said Zeus.

"Will you destroy it?"

"Not I," said Zeus.

"What will you do?" asked Poseidon.

"I will send my winds," said Zeus. "And you will help me raise a storm at sea. Then watch and you will understand the will of Zeus."

. . . .

MEDEA'S TRICK

The storm of the gods lashed the sea into a frenzy. It scattered ships across the Mediterranean and blew one special ship to Crete. That ship was the singing Argo, which was carrying Jason, a heroic warrior, to his home in Greece.

Jason was returning from the Quest for the Golden Fleece. Aeetes, the sorcerer king, had tried to stop Jason from finding the Fleece. He had challenged Jason to plow a field with his two fiery bulls and then to plant fifty serpent's teeth. Jason accepted the challenge. He forced the fiery bulls to plow the field and planted the serpent's teeth. The serpent's teeth sprang out of the earth as warriors that attacked him. Jason tricked the warriors into attacking each other, and they were all killed. That night, Jason found the secret path into the Midnight Garden of the Dragon. He lulled the dragon to sleep and took the Golden Fleece.

Jason was called a hero for all these deeds, but it was Medea who had shown him what to do every time. Medea was King Aeetes' daughter, a beautiful witch who knew even darker magic than her father. She had joined Jason on his voyage home and protected him from every danger. Yet, even Medea could not stop the storm from blowing Jason's ship to Crete.

From the deck of the Argo, Jason and his men stared in astonishment at the Bronze Giant on the shore. At first, they thought he was a colossal statue. Then, he lifted a boulder and threw it at them. The boulder soared toward them like a comet and tore through their sail.

The magic voice of Jason's ship wailed out, "Death and defeat! Turn back!"

"Turn the ship!" Jason shouted. But another boulder struck and broke the ship's rudder, so that it could not be steered at all. "We cannot escape," Jason cried, and he drew his sword out of its scabbard. "We must fight the giant."

"You cannot pierce that wall of bronze," Medea said. "No man can defeat him."

"What can we do, Medea?" Jason asked.

"Lower the rowboat," she answered. "A woman will fight that man of metal."

Medea raised her arms. She paused and bowed her head as if to summon some secret power deep within her. When she lifted her head, her eyes were cold and distant. She began to sing eerie words in a high and haunting voice. It made the men forget their fear and drop their weapons, as if in a dream. Silently, they lowered the rowboat into the sea.

Still singing, Medea climbed down the ship's ladder and boarded the rowboat. She did not touch the oars, yet the boat moved steadily over the waves toward the giant on the shore.

Talus heard her singing and dropped his boulder. Medea's voice wove around him. At first the sounds of her song seemed like many silken threads, then like many paths that crossed and criss-crossed in a thousand different directions. The giant tried to follow each one in his mind, but he felt more and more confused.

Suddenly, the song stopped, and he saw that Medea was standing directly in front of him, gazing into his eyes.

"Do you like my song?" she asked in a voice that remained strangely musical.

"It is beautiful," said Talus. For the first time, the giant felt beauty.

"Are you a god?" she asked.

"No," he replied. "I am Talus. A god made Talus, but Talus is not a god. Talus lasts a thousand years, but Talus does not last forever."

"That is sad," she said.

"Yes," he said. For the first time, the giant felt sadness.

"What makes you last so many years?" she asked.

"The gods put a liquid called *ichor* in my veins. It keeps Talus alive."

Medea said, "You are not alive, Talus. You are a machine, and the ichor is merely fuel to keep you working. Let me pour out the ichor and fill you with life. I will make you live forever."

For the first time, the giant felt happiness. "Do it," he said, pointing to a bronze plug in his right ankle. "This holds in the ichor," he said.

Medea pulled the plug and a silvery liquid spurted out. As it drained into the sand, Medea sang about Talus in a wondrous voice that sounded like a thousand different voices. Her song described the giant's strength and his many mighty battles; even how he had attacked Jason's ship with his boulders and how Medea had left the ship and come to meet Talus on the shore.

Suddenly her voice became low and harsh as she sang these words:

> *All living things must turn to dust.*
> *All metal things must turn to rust.*
> *All things must end someday.*

She sang the words again. This time Talus felt frightened, as if the sounds were weaving around his throat and tightening.

He tried to raise his arms and shout, *No more singing!* But he was so weak that he fell to his knees.

Medea sang the words a third and final time.

> *All living things must turn to dust.*
> *All metal things must turn to rust.*
> *All things must end someday.*

37

The giant
could only
whisper, "Medea, almost all the ichor has drained
away. Fill Talus with life."

Medea sneered and answered him in words as cold as ice. "I gave
you life already. I showed you beauty, sadness and happiness. You
felt more life in those few moments than you have felt in a thousand
years."

The giant fell face forward in the sand. He groaned, "You
promised to make Talus live forever."

Medea replied, "I will tell your story. I will tell about
your strength and your many mighty battles. I will tell how
you tried to sink our ship and kill us all. Then, I will tell how
I tricked you and destroyed you instead. Your story will never
be forgotten. The name of Talus will live forever."

Medea turned away. She boarded the rowboat, which glided
across the water toward the ship where Jason and his men were
waiting.

As the Bronze Giant lay motionless, the tide came in, wave after
wave, breaking his body apart; and the pieces began to rust.

King Minos was in his palace when a messenger brought him
the news about Talus. The king turned pale and threw down his
peacock crown. He ran to his horse and chariot, yelling at the
messenger, "You're a madman or a liar! The Bronze Giant cannot die.
It's impossible!"

Minos drove wildly out of the palace, calling out for Talus,
demanding that he rouse himself and return to duty.

Beneath the sea, Zeus asked Poseidon, "Did you watch and understand?"

"What you said came true," said Poseidon. "Talus was your gift. You did
not take him back or destroy him. But King Minos lost him because of you."

Zeus nodded, saying, "That was the will of Zeus." 🔱

THE GREAT WHITE BULL

THE GREAT WHITE BULL

A GIFT FROM THE SEA

KING MINOS RUSHED TO THE SEASHORE. The Bronze Giant that had protected Crete for centuries now lay in pieces on the sand.

The people blamed the king. "You angered the god Zeus," they said. "He destroyed the giant to punish you."

The king shouted back, "The Bronze Giant doesn't matter! You don't need him any more. He protected you when Crete was weak, but now Crete is powerful. It has ninety cities and a thousand ships that rule the sea. And Crete has me, the great King Minos!"

The people said, "You do not deserve to be our king."

Minos' two brothers stepped forward.

They said, "We should rule Crete instead of you."

King Minos frowned at them and answered, "Let the gods show us who should be king."

Minos did not pray to Zeus. He knew that Zeus would not help him. Instead, he stepped into the waves and whispered, "Poseidon, God of the Sea, if you help me, I will worship you above all the gods, even above Zeus."

The sea churned. White waves rolled in, beating against the rocks like stamping hooves. Then, a single massive wave came rolling out of the sea. It crashed like thunder on the shore and when it washed away, a great white bull was standing in its place. The bull lowered its head and Minos, seeing its huge sharp horns, began to back away, fearing that the bull was going to charge. Instead, the bull approached him meekly and knelt at his feet.

Minos hid his relief with an arrogant smirk and announced to the people, "Behold! The bull has bowed to me. The gods have sent me this creature as proof that I am the true king of Crete."

The people cheered. They shouted, "The gods have chosen Minos!" His two brothers scowled and turned away. They would have to leave the island and find other realms to rule. Minos remained the king of Crete.

. . . .

POSEIDON'S FURY

King Minos built a shrine to glorify the god, Poseidon. He started a festival where gymnasts leapt over Poseidon's bull, while others danced around it, tossing flowers.

The people agreed, "The gods gave Minos the finest bull that ever lived. It proves that he is meant to rule the island."

That night, after the festival, King Minos heard Poseidon's voice in the roar of the sea. "The Great White Bull is mine. Sacrifice the bull to me."

Minos would not listen. "I cannot give it up," he said. "It is living proof of my greatness."

He sacrificed a different bull instead.

The next night, Poseidon called to him again from the sea, "Sacrifice the bull to me."

Minos sacrificed a dozen other bulls, but he would not give up the Great White Bull.

On the third night, Poseidon sent a storm that battered the island, knocking down trees and ripping off roofs. An hour before dawn, the earth began to quake. Everyone was terrified, even Queen Pasiphae, the wife of King Minos.

"Go back to sleep," Minos told her. "The god's anger will not last."

But the god's anger grew worse. Poseidon filled the Great White Bull with a mad fury. The beast bellowed and kicked and broke out of its pen. It charged through the palace doors, then down the Great Hall, destroying everything in its path. When it came to the royal bedroom, it smashed the door and burst into the room. The palace shook with the roar of the bull and the screams of the queen.

44

By the time the guards arrived, the bull was gone. Queen Pasiphae lay on the floor, paralyzed with terror.

The king rushed to the balcony. He shouted to the sea, "I give up! I will sacrifice the Great White Bull!"

"Too late," came a voice out of the waves that crashed upon the distant shore. "Too late!"

In the spring, Queen Pasiphae gave birth. When the baby emerged, it did not cry. It was as silent as its horrified mother. King Minos stared and moaned. The baby had the head of a bull.

THE PUZZLE OF DAEDALUS

THE PUZZLE OF DAEDALUS

Q UEEN PASIPHAE GAVE BIRTH TO A MONSTER, a baby with the head of a bull. They called it the Minotaur.

"This is my fault," King Minos cried. "The god Poseidon ordered me to sacrifice his Great White Bull, but I would not give it up. Now Poseidon has punished us with this horror."

The queen could not touch the creature. It looked too much like Poseidon's bull that had terrified her in the night so many months before. Her fear of the bull had haunted her, especially in her sleep. It had been her constant nightmare. Now, it was her child.

The Minotaur cried for its mother. Queen Pasiphae could not go near it. Its cries grew loud and angry. The queen locked herself in her room. Its cries became a roar.

Queen Pasiphae abandoned her bull child. She even abandoned the palace. So did all the servants. King Minos was left with only his guards. Yet, none of them could control the beast. It grew quickly and broke everything in its reach. It beat its head against the walls and doors. It stamped its feet and bellowed day and night.

The king called in priests, doctors and magicians to calm the beast, but it grew even wilder. Finally, Daedalus the Inventor offered his help.

"It is hopeless," said the king. "I have tried everything."

"Not everything," said Daedalus. "You have tried prayers, medicines and magician's tricks. You have not tried to use the power of my intelligence."

King Minos said, "If you are so intelligent, then solve this problem. The Minotaur has royal blood, so it cannot be forced to leave the palace. It cannot be hurt, chained or locked up, but it must be controlled. Tell me, how can it be controlled?"

Daedalus bowed to the king. He said, "Your problem intrigues me. I cannot resist a good riddle." And he left.

47

Three days later, Daedalus returned. "I have the answer," he said. "This is how you can control the Minotaur." He handed the king a seashell with a spiral shape. "Do you see the winding path inside this shell?" he asked.

"Yes," said the king. "But I cannot see where the path ends."

Daedalus nodded, "Yes, but imagine if I made some more openings in this spiral shell. Imagine if I took hundreds of shells and made openings in all of them. What if I connected all the shells together? Hundreds of openings would connect to hundreds of other openings. Hundreds of paths would connect to hundreds of other paths. Could you ever find the way out of such a complicated puzzle?"

King Minos became angry, "I don't want a puzzle. I want an answer!"

Daedalus replied with a smile, "The puzzle is your answer. I will control the Minotaur by keeping him inside a puzzle. I will not build the puzzle out of shells. I will build it out of full-sized rooms, hundreds of rooms. My puzzle will be a huge dark maze underneath the palace."

"Why would you build it there?" asked King Minos.

Daedalus answered, "It will solve your problem. The maze will be part of the palace, so you will not have to force the Minotaur to leave. The Minotaur will not be hurt, chained or locked up. Yet it will be controlled, because it will never find the way out."

King Minos shook his head. "That would be heartless," he said. "The Minotaur must stay here with me. My guards will control it."

Suddenly, they heard a scream from a distant room. They rushed through the halls and found a guard sprawled upon the floor, with his double-edged axe lying useless at his side. The Minotaur had torn out the guard's throat and, covered in blood, was crouched over his body.

The king turned pale. He gave the order to Daedalus, "Build your maze. Let the maze control the monster."

Daedalus built a maze made out of hundreds of rooms. He marked the walls with the symbol of the Royal Family of Minos, the double-edged axe, which can still be seen on those walls today. The Minotaur was left in the center of the maze, never to escape. Daedalus called his maze the Labyrinth. ♆

49

THE DEADLY QUEST OF ANDROGEUS

THE DEADLY QUEST OF ANDROGEUS

A FATAL PROMISE

POSEIDON, GOD OF THE SEA, HAD GIVEN THE GREAT WHITE BULL TO KING MINOS. Poseidon had later demanded that the king sacrifice the bull. When the king would not give it up, Poseidon caused the bull to go mad. The beast wrecked the palace. It then attacked and terrified Queen Pasiphae, who later gave birth to the monstrous Minotaur. The Great White Bull rampaged through the land, trampling everything and everyone in sight.

Androgeus, the eldest son of King Minos and Queen Pasiphae, stood on the highest balcony of the palace. He gazed across the countryside. "I am going to find that bull and bring it back," he said.

King Minos warned him, "That beast cannot be stopped by anyone except a great hero."

"That's right," Androgeus answered. "When I capture it, everyone will call me a great hero."

King Minos shook his head. "You are hardly more than a boy," he said. "I have sent Hercules to capture it."

Androgeus turned red—first with shame, then with anger. He said, "If Hercules fails, promise that you will let me try."

King Minos laughed.

"I will," he said.

But Minos had a secret. He knew that Hercules had already caught the bull. Nevertheless, he told his son, "If Hercules cannot stop the Great White Bull once and for all, then I will let you try."

"Thank you, Father," said Androgeus. "I will make you proud of me."

King Minos hurried to his throne room. He had to prepare for the bull's return. He removed his crown of peacock feathers and put on the horned mask of a priest. He would sacrifice the bull to Poseidon, as he should have done long before.

King Minos waited all night, but Hercules did not return with the bull.

A week later a message arrived from Hercules: "I have taken the bull to Greece. I owed a debt to King Eurystheus and I have paid my debt by presenting him with the Great White Bull."

Minos was furious. He sent his servants with a strongbox filled with gold to buy back the bull, but they arrived too late. The bull had escaped. It had broken from its chains. It had burst through its fences and its walls. Nothing and no one could stop it.

"I can stop it," Androgeus told his father.

"You cannot," said King Minos. "It is too dangerous."

"You have already given me permission, Father," Androgeus said.

"I did not," he answered. "I said you could try to capture the bull only if Hercules failed to stop it. He did stop it."

"Don't try to trick me," Androgeus said. "You said, 'If Hercules cannot stop the Great White Bull once and for all, then I will let you try.' Hercules only stopped the bull once. I will stop it *once and for all*."

Androgeus walked out of the palace and mounted his father's chariot.

"Where are you going?" his father called to him.

"My friends are waiting for me at the port," replied Androgeus. "We have a ship and we are setting sail for Greece."

"You're too young. You don't know what you are doing!" his father shouted.

Androgeus waved goodbye. "I am a man now. Soon, I will be a hero," he said.

. . . .

THE SACRIFICE

When Prince Androgeus arrived in Athens, the city was crowded with athletes who had come for the Great Games. Androgeus joined them. He raced and wrestled. He threw the discus and the spear. He won every competition and received Athens' highest awards, the Crown of Laurels of Apollo and the Olive Branch of Athena. As the crown was placed upon his head, he raised the olive branch and shouted to the cheering crowd, "Now, I will win an even greater prize. I am going to capture the Great White Bull."

The crowd fell silent.

Aegeus, King of Athens, put his hand upon the young man's shoulder and said, "Androgeus, don't throw your life away."

Androgeus replied, "I am not afraid of any bull. In Crete, we worship Poseidon, God of the Sea and Herder of Bulls. We capture wild bulls every spring. We leap and dance around them at our festivals and crown our houses with their horns. We sacrifice the best ones to Poseidon."

"Don't sacrifice your life to be a hero," said the King of Athens. "The god does not need your blood."

Androgeus merely laughed.

The next day, he and his friends set out to find the bull. They followed its trail to the Plain of Marathon and found a pond where they knew the bull would come to drink. They set up a decoy, a model of a cow, constructed by Daedalus the Inventor. And they hid nearby.

The bull was fooled. It approached the decoy, thinking it was a real cow. It did not see the net that had been set next to the decoy. As the bull stepped into the net, Androgeus pulled its ropes tight and the young men rushed out of their hiding places to help.

The Great White Bull was trapped—until its anger exploded. It rushed across the field, dragging the young men by their ropes until each one fell away. It then turned and lowered its deadly horns, ready to charge the young men. Their only hope of escape was to climb a tree, but the nearest tree was at the top of a steep hill.

"Run for the tree!" yelled Androgeus.

They ran, but Androgeus did not follow. Instead he stood in the path of the bull and seized it by its horns.

His friends climbed the tree with tears in their eyes, for they knew the prince was sacrificing his life for them. Their hearts sank as they heard Androgeus' screams.

Soon they heard the Great White Bull bellow in triumph. The young men could not bear to look. Instead they faced east, toward the sea, and prayed to Poseidon that their good friend would be rewarded for his courageous death.

Poseidon granted their prayers, and the spirit of Androgeus was guided to the Underworld.

Once there, he was led to the Elysium Fields, where only the most brave and noble find their final home. As he entered, the spirits of all the great heroes rose to welcome Androgeus as one of their own.

54

THESEUS AND THE MINOTAUR

THESEUS AND THE MINOTAUR

THE MINOTAUR'S REVENGE

THE FRIENDS OF PRINCE ANDROGEUS RETURNED TO CRETE WITH HEAVY HEARTS. They could barely speak above a whisper when they told King Minos that his son had been killed trying to capture the Great White Bull.

King Minos gripped the arms of his throne and fell into a stony silence. No one dared to move or even to look at one another.

Finally the king spoke with cold and bitter anger. "The Athenians are to blame. They were jealous of my son, and they were afraid he would conquer them. They tricked him somehow so the bull would kill him."

"It was no one's fault," said the friends. "Androgeus did his best, but the bull was too powerful."

King Minos would not listen. "I lost my son. Someone must pay," he said.

Suddenly they heard a roar beneath their feet. The Minotaur was raging in his Labyrinth under the palace.

"Listen to that," said King Minos. "The Minotaur knows that its brother is dead. It is calling for revenge."

On that very day, King Minos formed a deadly plan and set it into motion. Crete had always been a peaceful island. But within a year, Minos rebuilt Crete's ships for war and trained Crete's sailors to be warriors. He then sailed his fleet of warships to Athens and blockaded the city, making sure no one could enter or escape.

The people of Athens began to starve and sicken. "We surrender," they cried. "Take what you want."

"I want revenge," said Minos. "Give me your finest young men and women. They shall face my other son, the Minotaur."

And so the Athenians were forced to agree that at each Great Year, which was every nine years, Athens would send fourteen of its finest young men and women to Crete, where they would be forced into the Labyrinth, never to be seen again.

. . . .

A POWERFUL YOUNG STRANGER

The Great White Bull continued to rage across the countryside, destroying crops and anyone who tried to stop it. But one day, a powerful young stranger stood in the bull's path. He wrestled it to the ground and broke its will. Then, he led the bull to Athens to sacrifice it—not to Poseidon, God of the Sea, but to Athena, Goddess of Wisdom.

The people asked the stranger, "Who are you? Where have you come from? Why are you here?"

The stranger answered, "My name is Theseus." But he would say no more.

All of Athens praised Theseus as a great hero, but no one knew his secret except Medea, who seemed to know every secret through her magic. Medea was the sorceress who had destroyed Talus, the Metal Giant, years before. She had ruined the life of Jason, a hero who had been foolish enough to trust her. From the moment she had arrived in Athens, she plotted to become its queen.

Medea had learned through her magic that a hero would one day challenge her power. The hero's name would be Theseus. She had watched and waited for him. She could sometimes glimpse him through the dark magic of her polished bronze mirror. She had seen him set out from Troezen and walk the long and dangerous route that followed the coast to Athens. She had seen his battles.

Periphetes the Clubber attacked him on a forest path, trying to smash his head with a huge brass club. Theseus was faster and stronger. He seized the club and used it on the Clubber.

Procrustes the Fitter tried to wrestle him into submission. Procrustes had defeated everyone he had ever challenged. When he won, he would tie his victim to one of his two horrible beds. He stretched some victims to death on his long bed. He used his axe to make others fit his short bed. Procrustes wrestled Theseus for a whole day, but Theseus proved too strong and too skilful. As the sun was setting, Procrustes could fight no longer. Theseus was finally able to drag him screaming to his fate. He fitted Procrustes first to his long bed and then to his short one.

Further down the road, Sinis, the Pine Bender, attacked Theseus. Sinis was a cruel killer who placed anyone he defeated between two young pine trees that he had bent to the ground. He tied his victim's arms to one tree and his victim's legs to the other. He would then release both trees at once and laugh as the trees sprang up, tearing his victim apart. Theseus defeated the Pine Bender and punished him with the terrible justice of the two pine trees.

The last villain was Sciron of the High Cliff. He would force his prisoners to kneel at the edge of a towering cliff and would order them to wash his feet. As they kneeled in front of him, he would kick them off the cliff into the churning sea. Theseus defeated Sciron, as well, and threw him from his own high cliff.

Medea saw all this and more of Theseus' adventures in her bronze mirror. She knew why he had faced those dangers and why he had captured the Great White Bull. Theseus was the secret son of King Aegeus of Athens. He was testing himself, proving that he could be a worthy son to the father he had never met. Medea scowled. If King Aegeus accepted him, Theseus would someday inherit the kingdom.

Medea looked once more into the mirror and saw Theseus sacrificing the Great White Bull at Athena's temple. She passed her hand across the mirror and turned it dark and dull. Medea no longer needed the mirror to watch him. She would soon be able to see Theseus through the palace window. The people were going to parade him through the streets. They would bring him to the palace.

Medea hurried to find King Aegeus. As she rushed through the halls, she murmured to herself, "I will never let Theseus have the kingdom. I will have it for myself."

She smiled as she entered the throne room. There was Old Aegeus, dozing on his throne. She had bewitched him into loving her and could make him do whatever she wanted. She leaned close to his ear and sang to him in her strange singsong voice.

59

Beware, beware of Theseus.
His smile's a knife.
His tongue's a snake.
He'll take your life
Before you wake.

"What? What?" The king awoke as if from a troubling dream.

"What is wrong, my king?" asked Medea.

"Theseus is dangerous. I have to stop him," he mumbled. "But I don't dare because the people love him."

"Welcome Theseus to the palace with a feast," Medea said in a spellbinding whisper. "I will put wolfsbane in his drink. It is the drool of Cerberus, the Three-Headed Hound of Hades, and a slow but deadly poison. It will burn him with a fever. It will choke him breath by breath. We will pretend to be worried. We will call every doctor. They will not know how to save him. He will die and we will cry for him. We will bury him with glory. Then we'll be safe and happy just like we were before."

"Whatever you say," King Aegeus mumbled. "You always know best."

A CUP OF TREACHERY

The king ordered a feast for Theseus and had the young hero sit on the right side of his throne.

"I come from the land of Troezen," said Theseus, speaking gently and looking deeply into the king's eyes. "Have you been to Troezen?"

The king began to remember.

"Troezen. Yes, I was in Troezen many years ago, when I was a young man like you. I loved a woman there. We were soon to have a child, but I was forced to leave and I could never return. That woman's eyes were hazel brown just like yours."

"Did you give her anything when you left?" asked Theseus.

"How did you know?" asked the king. "The day I left, I gave her my sword and sandals. I put them under a boulder that no one but I could lift. I told her that if someday our son grew strong enough to lift that boulder, he should carry the sword and put on the sandals. He should walk the long dangerous journey overland to Athens. If he survived, he could come to me and claim his rights as my only child."

Medea interrupted them. "Stop talking about the past! It's dead and over with."

She handed Theseus the poisoned cup and continued, "The king and I will soon be married. Will you raise your cup and drink to our happiness?"

Theseus raised his cup to Medea. "I wish that you get everything that you deserve," he said. "I have even brought a gift."

He drew his sword and placed it on the table between Medea and King Aegeus. They both began to tremble, but each for a different reason.

The king cried out in joy. "That handle has two golden snakes. It is the sword I left in Troezen for my son!"

Medea was shaking with anger. "Don't believe it," she snarled. "I have seen other swords just like it."

The king did not listen to her. Medea's spell was broken. He grabbed the cup from Theseus and said, "Your drink is deadly poison." Then, pointing at Medea, he said, "And that witch is even deadlier."

Medea summoned a wild wind that roared in through the windows and blew out all the torches. Hidden by the darkness and confusion, she hurried from the room and quickly gathered the treasures of the king. Before anyone could stop her, she flew away in a chariot pulled by dragons.

King Aegeus told Theseus, "Let her go. You are the only treasure I care about. You are my son and someday you shall be king."

. . . .

THESEUS SAILS TO CRETE

Theseus was Athens' greatest hero. He cleared the land of bandits. He caught the Great White Bull. He freed his father, King Aegeus, from the black magic of Medea. Yet the people still lived in fear.

The Athenians were compelled to send fourteen young men and women to King Minos every nine years as long as the Minotaur was living. The fourteen youths were taken to Crete and forced into the Labyrinth to face the murderous Minotaur.

"That monster will not kill again," said Theseus. "Not unless it kills me first."

When the next sacrifice was due, Theseus joined the young men and women who had been chosen to satisfy the beast, and together they set sail for Crete.

The winds blew fair and steady. Far sooner than they wished, they sailed into Crete's main port on the southern part of the island and were surrounded by warships. King Minos stood on the deck of the lead ship with a hundred warriors and the entire royal family.

"Theseus, my spies have told me all about you," said King Minos. "You are a fool to come here. You cannot survive the Minotaur. Even if you do, you cannot escape the Labyrinth. And even if you could escape it, you would never outrun my thirty warships."

Before Theseus could respond, a bolt of lightning flashed across the sky.

King Minos sneered and said, "The God of the Sky is threatening you."

Theseus replied, "Perhaps he is welcoming me."

King Minos glared.

63

He asked, "Will the God of the Sea also welcome you?"

With that, he pulled off his royal ring and tossed it into the sea, saying, "Let the god Poseidon help you find my ring."

Without a word, Theseus dove into the sea. Long minutes passed as everyone on board watched carefully for him to emerge, but not even a bubble broke the surface. Finally, the king announced, "No man can last that long underwater. Theseus has drowned."

A moment later, Theseus rose to the surface surrounded by a circle of chattering dolphins. He held up the ring and a golden crown as well.

He called out, "The dolphins led me to your royal ring. They also brought me this crown."

Theseus boarded Minos's ship and approached King Minos' two beautiful young daughters, Phaedra and Ariadne. Phaedra smiled kindly at him, and Theseus wanted to give her the crown. But a mysterious voice sang inside his mind:

Not her, not now
This time, this crown
Belongs to Ariadne.

Theseus bowed to Ariadne and presented the crown to her.

King Minos was furious, but he controlled his anger with a false smile and said, "This does not prove that Poseidon cares for Theseus. Not at all! This clearly proves that Poseidon is on my side. Look how the god has saved my ring and has sent my daughter a godly gift."

No one believed the king. Theseus smiled and Ariadne blushed.

. . . .

IN THE LABYRINTH

Princess Ariadne stared at the crown that had come from the sea.

She wondered, *Why did the dolphins bring this crown to Theseus? Why did Theseus give it to me?*

That night, a handsome young god came to her in a dream. She did not know who he was, but he wore a crown exactly like the one she had been given. He sang to her in a wondrous voice:

Help Theseus. Join Theseus
For love and for happiness
For ever.

Ariadne woke up, but her dream stayed with her. She kept herself busy with friends and family, but the young god remained in her thoughts and in her heart. Finally, she went to see Theseus, who was being closely guarded.

She whispered to him so the guards would not hear. "A god has sent me. I will help you kill the Minotaur, but you must take me with you when you escape from Crete."

Theseus quickly agreed and said, "I will fight the Minotaur by myself, but how can I get out of the Labyrinth?"

Ariadne handed Theseus a wooden box. She explained, "When I was a little girl, Daedalus the Inventor promised to answer one question, if I promised never to ask him another. I asked him for the secret way out of the Labyrinth. This box contains his answer."

Theseus opened the box. It held a ball of fine silk thread.

. . . .

The next night, Ariadne brought the guards wine laced with a sleeping potion. Within moments, they dropped like stones upon the ground. Ariadne took their keys and freed Theseus and his companions.

She led them to the Labyrinth and tied the end of the thread to the entrance. She told Theseus, "Unravel this thread as you search the Labyrinth for the Minotaur. If all goes well, you can follow the thread back here."

Ariadne gave Theseus a sword and watched him disappear into the darkness. She and the others waited for hours, gazing into the darkness of the maze and listening for his return. All they heard was a low wind moaning through empty passageways.

Suddenly, there was a terrible roar from deep inside the Labyrinth. It stopped as suddenly as it began, and there was only silence for the long fretful hours until dawn. As the sun began to rise, the thread on the ground tightened.

Was it Theseus? they wondered. *Or was it the beast?*

Ariadne heard a distant panting and heavy awkward footsteps. Then, out from the gloom of the maze, she saw a shape coming toward her—not huge and hulking, but tall and slim. It was Theseus, pulling on the thread as he followed it back to her. He was out of breath and limping badly.

"The Minotaur knocked the sword out of my hand, and I lost it in the dark," Theseus said. "I gripped the beast by its horns, knowing that if I let go, it would gore me to death. We wrestled in the dust, but I held on. I kept beating it with my bare fists, until I managed to get my arms around its throat. Then I choked the life out of it."

66

Ariadne gently touched Theseus' bruised and bloodied face.

"The monster is dead," she said. "Athens will never have to send another sacrifice to Crete. But there's no more time to talk. We must all flee before the guards awaken."

They rushed to the port. Before they set sail, however, Theseus and his crew boarded each of King Minos' warships. They smashed holes through the hulls, so the ships would sink and Minos would not be able to pursue them. As the last of Minos' ships filled with water, the young Athenians cheered.

Theseus laughed and declared, "If Minos wants to catch us, he'll have to swim! Come on, we're heading home to Athens!"

. . . .

ARIADNE'S CROWN

Theseus escaped from Crete, taking Princess Ariadne with him just as he had promised. Yet she cried bitter tears, because she knew her father would not forgive her and she could never return home. Theseus tried his best but could not comfort her.

On their voyage to Athens, they stopped at the island of Naxos to find fresh water. Ariadne wandered down the empty beach and cried once more, as she thought of everyone and everything she would never see again. Exhausted, she fell asleep in the sand. She did not hear Theseus and the others calling her.

A sudden storm was pushing their ship against the rocks; they had to pull away from shore before the ship was wrecked. As they entered deeper water, the storm drove their ship northward. Theseus fought hard against the winds, trying to return for Ariadne, but the storm blasted the black-sailed ship farther and farther across the sea. The wild winds would not cease, or even weaken, till they blew the ship to Athens.

Ariadne woke up and realized she was alone. "This is my punishment for being a fool," she cried. "I believed a dream. I listened to a god whose name I do not even know."

She kept crying as the storm moved off and the wind slowly calmed to a gentle breeze. For a long while, she could do nothing more than listen to the beating of the surf upon the sand, as if it were the beating of her own unhappy heart.

Then she heard a distant sound, the chant of women's voices singing, "Dionysus! Dionysus!"

Ariadne wiped away her tears and looked down the wind-swept beach. She saw a crowd of women coming closer, dancing joyfully along the foaming surf that crashed upon the sand. They were following goat-like men who were playing wild music on reed pipes. Ariadne called out to the women, but they didn't seem to notice her.

They kept singing "Dionysus! Dionysus!" as they danced with their arms raised high around a tall figure driving a chariot.

Ariadne rushed down the beach and joined the crowd, but not one of them stopped singing or dancing. They had eyes only for the man in the chariot. She pushed her way into the crowd, but she still could not see his face. Then, he turned and gazed at her. She felt dizzy, and for a moment she thought she would faint. He was the handsome young god from her dream.

The music and singing seemed to fade as the god Dionysus spoke. "Ariadne, why are you unhappy?"

She answered, "You told me to help Theseus and to follow him. You said I would find love and happiness forever."

He told her gently, "You will find it if you know how to ask for it. Do you want me to bring Theseus back?"

"No," she answered.

"What do you want?" he asked.

Ariadne thought deeply, then spoke her secret desire. "I want to be with you," she said. "I have wanted that ever since I saw you in my dream."

Dionysus stepped down from his chariot and took her hand.

"Now you have found love and happiness—and so have I," he said. "Your dreams are powerful, Ariadne. Each night, in sleep, you searched for someone you could truly love. Your dreams reached me, though I was in India, a land far to the east. They drew me to you. I crossed mountains and rivers, forests and lakes and finally found you. But I did not know how to reveal myself.

"When I saw Theseus arriving in Crete, I decided that he could help us and we could help him. When Theseus dove into the sea, I sent him a crown to give to you. That night, as you slept holding the crown in both your hands, I showed myself to you in a dream. I asked you to help by following Theseus. When you did, you showed me that you believed in the dream I sent you as much as I believed in the dreams that you sent me.

"Everything that happened after that was meant to bring you here to me. I knew that you would stop at this island and that the storm would drive off the ship. I waited here for you, so we could meet in this way."

Ariadne felt herself glowing as Dionysus led her through the crowd to his chariot.

"Dionysus," she said, "this is better than any dream."

Dionysus gave her a crown with seven Indian rubies.

"Wear this at our wedding," he told her. "It is more glorious than the crown I sent you from the sea, and it will last as long as love itself."

They were married that very night.

Together, Dionysus and Ariadne held the crown of rubies up to the moonless sky, and it became a constellation of seven stars that will shine forever. Some call it the *Corona Borealis*. Others call it *Ariadne's Crown*.

THE FLIGHT OF DAEDALUS AND ICARUS

THE FLIGHT OF DAEDALUS AND ICARUS

K ING MINOS WAS FURIOUS. Theseus had killed the Minotaur and escaped from the Labyrinth. He had sunk the king's ships and sailed off with the king's daughter.

King Minos knew he would never catch Theseus.

"Daedalus the Inventor must take the blame for this," said Minos. "He built the Labyrinth. He alone knew the secret way to escape it. He must have helped Theseus."

King Minos shouted to his guards, "Arrest Daedalus. Throw him and his son into the Labyrinth. Seal them inside forever!"

Daedalus was listening from a passageway that he had secretly built under the floor of the palace. He heard every word the king had said. He and his son, Icarus, followed the passageway out of the palace and escaped into the open fields.

Icarus wanted to stop and face their enemies.

"Let us fight and die like noble heroes," he said.

Daedalus answered, "Let's run away and live like clever men."

"We can't escape," said Icarus. "The king has thousands of soldiers and sailors. They will catch us wherever we go, on the land or on the sea."

"Correct," said Daedalus, "but they cannot catch us in the air. We will escape into the sky."

Daedalus had invented many things: the carpenter's level, the compass, even the umbrella. This time he had to create his most important invention. Their lives depended on it.

Working quickly in a hidden workshop, Daedalus built two pairs of wings larger than the wings of eagles. He covered them with feathers glued on with beeswax. He and his son carried the wings to a windy cliff above the sea. Daedalus attached a stiff bar across each pair of wings, for strength and support, and showed Icarus how to strap himself to the bar.

He said, "The wind is blowing strong and steady. We will glide all the way to Greece. Watch me and follow me. Do exactly what I do."

73

Daedalus lifted his wings. He balanced them on his shoulders, ran to the edge of the cliff and leaped. For a moment it looked as if he would fall, but his wings held him and carried him on the wind.

Icarus followed eagerly. He called out, "I'm flying!"

"You are like a bird," said Daedalus.

"Better than a bird!" he shouted back. "I am like a god."

"But you are not a bird and you are not a god," Daedalus warned him. "You are a boy who has much to learn. Do not fly too high. Do not fly too low. Both are dangerous. Follow the middle way."

Icarus obeyed.

For many hours, father and son glided above the sea. At one point, they flew over a ship. Icarus laughed as the sailors on board dropped to their knees.

One called out, "Monsters! Birdmen!"

The rest yelled, "They are gods! Pray to them!"

After hours of flying over the sea, Icarus grew bored. He looked up at the sun and spoke his thoughts out loud, "Apollo, God of the Sun, is driving his fiery chariot across the sky. Perhaps I can reach him. If I can prove that I can fly as high as a god, he may welcome me. He may lead me to Mount Olympus and let me join the gods."

Just then Icarus entered a current of hot air that was rising from a desert island. The hot air pushed him upward.

Daedalus shouted, "Don't let it lift you any further. Dip your wings. Fly down to me."

Icarus would not listen. Instead, he raised one wing high and dipped the other wing low. He turned in a circle and rose higher with the rising air.

"Too high! Too high!" Daedalus shouted, but Icarus could barely hear him. He was spiralling up so swiftly that his father sounded like a bird crying far beneath him.

"Higher! Higher!" Icarus yelled, cheering

h i m s e l f
upward, rising
toward the sun.
He did not feel
the wax melting in
the heat. He did not
see the feathers dropping
off.

Suddenly, he was falling,
tumbling through the air. He
tried to call out, "Father,
help!" But his words twisted
into a scream.

. . . .

77

Daedalus found his son's
body floating with the wreckage of
his wings. He buried Icarus on a
nearby island, which he named
Icaria.

As Daedalus stood beside the grave,
a ship passed close by. It was the same
one they had flown over earlier that day.

The sailors called out to Daedalus, "We
saw two gods flying in the sky!"

Daedalus shook his head
sadly. "They were not gods,"
he answered. "You saw a
foolish boy who flew
too high up and fell too far
down. And you saw a helpless
father who could not teach his son the
middle way."

KING MINOS SEEKS REVENGE

KING MINOS SEEKS REVENGE

A FLAME IN THE NIGHT SKY

DAEDALUS, THE GREAT INVENTOR AND ARCHITECT, WAS A HUNTED MAN. MINOS, King of Crete, had built a new fleet of warships and sworn an oath that he would never stop his search for Daedalus—not until he found and killed him for revealing the secret of the Labyrinth.

The King of Cumae in Italy offered Daedalus a safe hiding place in return for building him something wonderful. Daedalus did not disappoint the king. He went to work immediately, constructing a magnificent temple with a brilliant golden roof dedicated to Apollo, God of the Sun and God of Intelligence. However, when King Minos came searching for him with his new warships, Daedalus fled to Egypt.

The Pharaoh of Egypt welcomed him as well for he also admired the inventor's skills. Daedalus knew how to impress even a pharaoh. He built a splendid temple to glorify Hephaestus, God of Fire—the Blacksmith God, who heated and beat metal in volcanoes to make weapons, jewellery and marvellous machines. Again King Minos discovered where Daedalus was hiding, and again Daedalus had to flee for his life.

In the dead of night, Daedalus flew high above the Mediterranean Sea on the wide wings he had invented. This time he did not know where to hide. He wanted to pray to Apollo, but it was dark. Apollo had driven his fiery chariot beyond the western shore. Daedalus was alone, lost in the night sky.

He called out to the god Hephaestus. "Great Hephaestus, I have built a temple to glorify your name. I have spent my life creating and inventing just like you. Will you protect me?"

An instant later, a flame blazed on the horizon. It was Mount Etna erupting on the island of Sicily.

Daedalus laughed with relief, "The god Hephaestus is signalling to me with the fire of his volcano!"

The volcano cooled and settled as Daedalus reached the island. He found his way to King Cocalus, ruler of Sicily, who was delighted to meet him.

"I have heard about your skills and your great inventions," said the king. "I've also heard about your troubles. You are welcome to stay here. You do not have to pay me with your work. We accept you freely as our guest."

Daedalus bowed to the king and answered, "I invent and build because I love to, not because I have to. Allow me to create wonderful things and I will always be happy here."

The king gave him a workshop and as many workers as he wanted. Daedalus built the king a palace and a fortress. And, for the people of Sicily, he built a public steam bath heated by Mount Etna's underground streams of lava.

. . . .

A SIMPLE TRICK

Just as Daedalus completed his work, King Minos sailed into the port with his black ships of war.

Daedalus pleaded with King Cocalus, "Do not let Minos know that I am here. I am too old to keep running away."

King Minos did not attack. Instead, he landed with a hundred servants carrying painted vases and golden goblets, wondrous woven cloth and tall clay jars of olive oil and wine.

A ragged old beggar hobbled toward Minos pleading, "Share your riches! Look at me. I am dirty and covered with sores. See how badly I need your help."

Minos pushed the beggar away, refusing even to glance at him. But he greeted King Cocalus with great warmth.

"My fellow king, I heard that you have just completed the most impressive palace ever built. I bring gifts to help you celebrate. Will you let me admire your palace?"

Cocalus was suspicious, but he was also flattered. He showed King Minos his palace, his fortress, even his public steam baths that were large enough for hundreds of his people to enjoy.

"Only a brilliant architect and engineer could create such wonders," said Minos.

Cocalus answered cautiously, "My kingdom has many brilliant architects and engineers. We Sicilians are all very intelligent."

"If you are so intelligent, can you solve a puzzle?" asked Minos.

"Certainly. What sort of a puzzle?" asked Cocalus who was feeling more and more uncertain.

Minos placed a spiral shell in Cocalus' hand and asked, "Can you wind a thread to the end of a spiral shell? I will give my royal ring to the one who can do it."

That night, King Cocalus, his family and all his advisors poked and pushed strings into the shell, but none of them could reach the end. Daedalus became more and more frustrated as he watched them fail so miserably.

Finally, he blurted out, "It's easy. It's obvious! It's just a simple trick!"

Daedalus drilled a small hole through the pointed end of the shell. Then he smeared honey outside the hole. He tied a thin thread to an ant and placed the ant inside the shell.

"Now watch," he said. "The ant will carry the string to the end."

The ant smelled the honey and went after it, searching deep into the shell. It reached the hole and crawled out to get the honey, pulling the thread after it.

"There it is," said Daedalus. "I've used this lowly creature to solve a royal problem."

Cocalus brought the shell to Minos and flaunted it before him. "There it is," he smirked. "I've solved the puzzle. It was just a simple trick."

Minos examined the thread winding through the shell.

"How very intelligent," he said with a sneer. "However, the real trick is on you, King Cocalus. You see, I have a name for this puzzle. I call it the Little Labyrinth. Only one person could find such a clever way to solve it, and that person is not you. It is Daedalus, who created my Labyrinth on Crete. Now I am certain he is here."

King Minos stood at the palace window and raised his hand so that his gold ring flashed in the sun, signalling to his army.

Hundreds of warriors swarmed out of his ships and quickly overran the palace.

"Search everywhere," Minos commanded. "Look for secret passages and hidden rooms. Daedalus is a genius; he will find the most complicated way to hide."

The warriors smashed through walls. They tore out floors and ceilings. They searched everywhere. But they could

not find anything unusual except for a mysterious spiral staircase that led down from the steam baths, deep into the earth.

Minos stared into the gloomy depths of the staircase, uncertain where it might lead. Just as he backed away, someone grabbed him by his arm. It was the old beggar again, the one who had annoyed him when he first arrived.

The beggar shook his filthy finger in Minos' face and warned him, "Do not descend that staircase. It leads down to the realm of the god Hephaestus. No one, not even Daedalus, would dare to disturb that god."

Minos stared suspiciously at the old man. "Daedalus must have sent you to frighten me away. But I am smarter than he thinks. Now I know where he is hiding."

King Minos and his men rushed down the spiral stairs. When they reached the bottom, they found a wall of black stone with an enormous face carved into it. It was the frowning face of Hephaestus.

"Daedalus must be hiding on the other side," said Minos. "Break through it."

"We do not dare!" the warriors said. "We must not strike a god."

"You superstitious fools! That face has no power," yelled Minos.

He grabbed a warrior's double-edged axe and struck the face. The carving cracked.

"See," Minos gloated. "It's nothing but stone."

The crack widened like a horrible grin, and then the face shattered. Steam hissed out. Minos had broken into the volcano.

"Out of my way!" Minos screamed. He scrambled past his men, desperate to escape. But it was too late. Scalding water, heated by the bubbling lava, gushed out and filled the spiral tunnel. Minos and his warriors were boiled alive.

Far above them, at the entrance to the staircase, the beggar listened to their dying screams. He removed his dusty cap. He dropped his ragged cloak. It was Daedalus in disguise. As he rubbed the dirt from his face, he spoke into the steaming hole.

"King Minos, you thought that I would use a complicated way to hide from you. However, sometimes the best trick is a simple trick." ꙮ

THE GIANT WAVE, THE CLOUD OF DEATH

THE GIANT WAVE, THE CLOUD OF DEATH

THESEUS WAS WOKEN BY A DISTANT EXPLOSION THAT SET ALL THE DOGS OF ATHENS BARKING. Hours later a giant wave rolled in from the south. It smashed ships against the shore and flooded half the city. A deadly cloud that covered Athens in ash and sulphur followed the wave. Birds suffocated in the sky and fell at Theseus' feet.

The people of Athens would soon be calling for his help. Theseus was the new king. It was up to him to protect the city. He paced back and forth inside his palace trying to understand what had caused this disaster. The giant wave and ash cloud had come from the direction of Crete, the island of King Minos and the Minotaur. Both Minos and the Minotaur were dead, but Crete was still powerful and dangerous. Phaedra, the daughter of King Minos, had become the new ruler.

Theseus wondered aloud, "Has Queen Phaedra sent this wave and cloud? Is she trying to conquer us like her father did?"

Standing on his balcony and gazing out to sea, Theseus wondered, *How could Queen Phaedra master such terrible powers?. Was she getting help from the gods? Or perhaps from Daedalus the Inventor?*

Theseus had been a fighter all his life. He had cleared the land of bandits. He had overcome the black magic of Medea and had freed his father from her spell. He had broken Crete's power over Athens by killing the Minotaur and sinking almost all of Crete's warships. When he returned from Crete, Theseus found that his father was dead and that he had become the new king. He immediately led his people into battle against their other enemies.

He conquered the Amazons, powerful women warriors, and then he defeated the wild Centaurs, who were half human and half horse. His people hailed him as their greatest hero and most powerful leader. But now he felt completely helpless. How could anyone defeat water and smoke?

Theseus summoned his most trusted messenger and told him, "Hurry to the god Apollo's temple at Delphi. Find the priestess and repeat these exact words: *A giant wave and a cloud of death have struck Athens from across the sea.* Ask the god Apollo, *What should King Theseus do?*"

The messenger rushed to Delphi, and when he returned he had a strange tale to tell. He bowed to Theseus and said: "I gave your message to the priestess. She turned without a word and entered Apollo's sacred cave. I followed her and watched as she sat suspended over a wide crack in the earth. Her eyes closed and her head drooped as she went into a trance. A moment later she called out your question in a trembling voice: *What should King Theseus do?* Smoke and steam rose out of the earth until they covered her like a swirling cloud. Then, I heard the words of Apollo coming through her:

> *A great land dies by cloud and wave.*
> *When all is lost, then you must save*
> *The one most knowing, loyal and brave.*"

Theseus did not know what Apollo's answer meant. He asked his best advisors, but no one could explain it.

Finally, Theseus declared, "I do not understand the god's advice, but I know what I must do. I must defend Athens. I will not wait for Crete to attack us with more clouds and waves. I will set sail and fight my enemy face to face."

. . . .

A DESPERATE PLAN

Theseus sailed to Crete with a dozen ships and all his warriors. He had a desperate plan. He and his warriors would sail full speed into the port and fight their way past Crete's fleet of warships. Then they would ground their ships against the shore, leap out and battle Crete's army as they headed to the palace, far inland. Once they reached the palace, they would have to face a thousand guards, break through the tall strong doors and try to capture the queen. There was little hope of success, but it was the only way to force Crete to surrender.

Theseus grasped his sword as the small, swift ships of Athens raced full sail toward battle. He was determined to fight without pause or hesitation, but as he entered the port, he was shocked at what he saw. There was no navy to fight. The few ships in sight were half sunk and smouldering in the water. Theseus and his warriors leapt ashore and saw that there was no army either.

Wherever they looked, they saw wrecked buildings, collapsed roofs and a layer of ash covering everything. They trudged knee-deep through the ash until they reached the palace. There, they found its huge bronze doors broken off their hinges. No one tried to stop them. The palace seemed utterly deserted.

Theseus led his men inside. The building was so magnificent that it took their breath away. They stared at the graceful pillars and lofty ceilings. They were astonished by the polished mosaic floors, inlaid with lifelike images of fish, dolphins and octopi that seemed to swim through the sea.

The walls were brilliantly painted with life-sized people: a group of girls laughing together, a gathering of noble ladies and gentlemen of the court, a line of servants carrying food and drink. One large wall showed daring young men and women leaping over a charging bull.

Yet there was not one living person to be seen within the palace. Only pictures.

Theseus sent his warriors to search the gardens outside, and he went on alone. As he entered the last room, he gazed with uncertainty at its far wall. It was painted with two giant gryphons, part lion and part eagle, which stood guard on either side of a white alabaster throne. On the throne was the pale appearance of a queen wearing a peacock feather crown. As Theseus looked more closely, he realized it was not a painting of the queen at all. It was Queen Phaedra herself.

She was sitting motionless and so deep in thought that she did not realize Theseus had entered. She hardly looked older than when Theseus had first seen her many years before, when he had come to fight the Minotaur.

At that time, King Minos had dared him to fetch a ring thrown into the sea, and Theseus dove into the waves. A pod of dolphins led him to the ring but, before he could swim back to the surface, the dolphins swirled around him with a golden crown that spun and sparkled before his eyes. Just as he grasped it in his hand, he heard a godlike voice say, "Theseus, give this to my lady." When Theseus reached the surface, he boarded the warship of King Minos and faced the two grown daughters of the king, Phaedra and Ariadne. Phaedra gazed at him with such compassion that Theseus was about to offer her the crown. But the mysterious voice he had heard beneath the sea sang inside his mind,

Not her, not now
This time, this crown
Belongs to Ariadne.

Theseus then bowed to Ariadne and gave the crown to her.

Since that day, so many years before, Theseus would often think about Phaedra and wonder what might have been if he had given the crown to her. Now Theseus only thought of Phaedra with anger.

He broke his silence and his words resounded through the royal chamber. "Queen Phaedra," he said. "I hoped that we would meet again, but not like this."

Queen Phaedra raised her eyes and saw Theseus staring at her, sword in hand. "Theseus, what are you doing here?" she asked.

Theseus shouted, "I have come to stop you, Phaedra. Why did you attack my kingdom with a wild wave and a deadly cloud?"

Phaedra gazed at him with deep sorrow. "Oh Theseus, we were attacked, not you," she answered. "That wave and cloud hit us with full force. You felt only their fading powers."

"But why? How?" asked Theseus.

Queen Phaedra continued, "My father, King Minos, offended the gods. They punished him by luring him to his death in far off Sicily," she said. "We thought the gods were satisfied when he died, but we were wrong. They must have wanted further revenge, because now they have destroyed his kingdom.

"The god, Hephaestus, woke his volcano on Kalliste, our island city to the north, the island you Athenians call Atlantis. The eruption blew it apart and most of it has sunk into the sea. The blast created a wave that drowned half of Crete, and a terrible cloud of burning ash has smothered what was left."

Theseus felt a rumble underneath his feet, as if a colossal creature were rampaging through the Underworld. The walls shook, the painted gryphons cracked, their feet crumbled into dust.

Phaedra showed no fear, only overwhelming sadness. "The god Poseidon sends his earthquakes. They grow stronger every hour."

She sighed and dropped her peacock crown onto the floor.

"Crete was a great nation," she said. "We were always peaceful, until my father forced the people to make war. We loved to race and to play sports in the fields. We loved songs and dances, tricks, games and clever words. We invented wonders and created beauty everywhere. This palace was a happy place, where our most wise and skilful people met to share all that they knew. I learned from all of them, but now all is lost."

"What were those last words you said?" Theseus asked.

Phaedra repeated, "Now all is lost."

Suddenly, Theseus recalled the words of the god Apollo:

> *A great land dies by cloud and wave.*
> *When all is lost, then you must save*
> *The one most knowing, loyal and brave.*

Theseus realized what the god wanted him to do.

"Phaedra," he said. "You are the one most knowing, loyal and brave. The gods do not want me to fight you. They want me to save you. Let me take you from here."

Phaedra shook her head slowly and answered, "I must and will stay here. This is the very place where all our kings and queens have sat and ruled. I am the last of them, so it is my duty to remain. I possess all their wisdom, beginning with the knowledge of Queen Europa, who first ruled Crete. Zeus carried her here from

89

across the sea. She taught the people of Crete how to be a great nation."

The earth shook again. A pillar smashed upon the floor. Theseus looked up to see cracks spreading across the ceiling like a maze. Soon it would come crashing down.

He said, "Phaedra, do you wish you could be more like Queen Europa?"

"Yes, I do," Phaedra answered.

"I'll grant your wish," he told her. "I'll carry you across the sea just like Zeus carried her."

Theseus pulled Phaedra from her throne and threw her over his shoulder. Before she could catch her breath, he carried her out of the room. At that same moment, the roof collapsed and masses of rubble came crashing down.

Theseus gripped Phaedra tightly, as he carried her through the palace halls. All around them, pillars were falling, walls were cracking. The crowds of people painted on the walls seemed to tremble as he ran past.

"You tricked me!" Phaedra cried.

Theseus yelled, "Zeus tricked Europa. She didn't like it either!" The blue mosaic floor split open at his feet, but Theseus leapt across the gap. The mosaic fish and dolphins quivered beneath him.

He just laughed and shouted, "The sea is getting rough!"

Moments later, Theseus rushed out of the palace doors and lay gasping with Phaedra on the ground. The earth heaved one more time. They watched in horror as the grand palace collapsed like a colossal house of cards.

Phaedra cried out, "You have not saved me, Theseus. I could have died as a queen. Now I am doomed to live as a beggar in a ruined land."

"Don't give up hope, Phaedra," Theseus said. "Let me take you across the sea to Athens. Be my queen and share your knowledge with my people. Then you will truly be as great as Europa was."

Phaedra sat quietly, thinking to herself while the dust swirled and slowly settled upon the wreckage of the palace.

Finally, she said, "The glory of Crete has ended. The glory of Athens has begun."

She held out her hand to Theseus. "Let us go to Athens and rule that land together."

DISCOVERING A LOST WORLD

The Final Tale

DISCOVERING A LOST WORLD

THIRTY-FIVE HUNDRED YEARS AFTER THE MINOAN CIVILIZATION WAS DESTROYED, barely a trace of its glory could be found. There were only some carved stones and bits of broken pottery poking out of the dirt.

It was 1894. An Englishman named Arthur Evans was walking through a marketplace in Athens, when he came across an antique shop selling odd-looking gemstones. Evans was an expert in the history of ancient lands, but he had never seen anything like these gems. As he examined them, he realized that they must have come from rings or brooches made thousands of years before.

Each stone was engraved with a different image as if to identify a different owner. There were beautiful engravings of young people at play, acrobats and bulls, palaces and sailing ships. Yet the palaces and ships did not look like any he had ever seen before—nor did the exotic clothing, nor the sports being played, nor any of the many strange designs that were cut into the gems. He wondered who had carved them. They could only have been created by some undiscovered or long-forgotten people.

Arthur Evans had been a mountain climber, a war reporter, a spy and even the head of a great museum. Now, as he examined the engravings on those gemstones, he decided to become something else: a treasure hunter. He would not hunt for gold and silver, rare weapons or priceless statues. He would hunt for a far greater treasure—the answer to the mystery of those ancient gems.

The antique dealer told Evans that the gems had been found on the island of Crete. A farmer had been digging deep in the earth when he had come across the ruins of an ancient building. As he uncovered the ruins, he found the gemstones.

Evans sailed to Crete. He met other farmers who had also found gemstones, each with a unique engraving. The farmers believed that the stones were magic and would protect their children from evil spirits.

"That's just superstitious nonsense," said Evans.

He was a scientific thinker, who did not believe in magic. However, he did believe that a highly skilled people had created those engravings.

Evans explored the island searching for signs of an ancient civilization. Eventually, he reached a cave high on the side of a mountain. Inside, he found a

93

stone altar that had been used for making sacrifices. This proved to Evans that he was on the right track.

Later, others would discover another part of the cave, one that had been sealed off for many centuries by fallen rocks. They cleared away the rocks and found a deep cavern with hundreds of miniature objects; gold replicas of double-edged axes, swords and bulls. The objects dated as far back as four thousand years. They had been placed there by ancient worshippers as gifts for the god Zeus.

Evans continued searching the island for more signs of a lost world. He heard about a farmer who had uncovered ancient walls. Evans bought the land all around the walls and hired workers to dig throughout the area. The deeper they dug, the more walls they found, until Evans realized that they had uncovered the ruins of a grand palace. It had once been a magnificent building, as big as Buckingham Palace. The workers found hundreds of rooms, which seemed to have collapsed during some terrible disaster. The rooms appeared to be part of a huge maze. The walls were marked with the symbol of a double-edged axe and there was evidence of bloody sacrifices. Evans had discovered the Palace of Knossos, which myths describe as the home of King Minos and the Minotaur.

94

Evans spent the rest of his life uncovering, restoring and studying the ruins. There were beautiful wall paintings of nobles and servants. One mural showed young men and women circling a charging bull, while one man gracefully leapt over its lowered horns. There was a grand chamber with an alabaster throne and wall paintings of gryphons. Sacred objects lay scattered on the floor. It looked as if the chamber had been suddenly abandoned at the time the palace was destroyed. The entire area had a thick layer of volcanic ash and evidence of fire and earthquakes.

One day, as the peasant workers were digging, an earthquake hit. It was so powerful that they were all thrown to the ground. The rocks under the earth began grinding against each other, making a terrible roar. When the earthquake ended, the peasants recalled ancient tales of giant bulls beneath the earth. They said the bulls had roared and made the earth quake.

Evans told them, "I am a man of science. I don't believe in giant bulls or minotaurs or ancient gods."

"Do you believe in Daedalus the Inventor?" a young peasant woman asked.

"That's just another myth," Evans answered.

"I've seen something Daedalus built," she said.

The young woman and her two sisters took Evans to a courtyard of the palace.

They told him, "Daedalus made a mosaic on this floor. It was shaped into an intricate path of coloured stones. Ariadne and Phaedra, the daughters of King Minos, would move along the winding path as they performed the Dance of the Cranes. Our people still do it."

The three sisters joined hands and performed the ancient folk dance.

Evans was impressed. "You dance so gracefully," he told them. "You are like the three Graces, the most lovely daughters of Zeus."

"So you do believe in the gods!" they laughed.

Evans blushed.

. . . .

THE END OF THE HUNT

Evans worked for forty years uncovering the palace and parts of the ancient city around it. He found 3,000 clay tablets written in an unknown language which is still not understood. He found wonderful works of art and engineering that proved that Crete had been one of the great civilizations of the world. Evans called it the Minoan Civilization after the mythical King Minos. He became famous for his discovery. He was knighted by the King of England and named Sir Arthur Evans.

When Sir Arthur grew very old, he decided to return to England. He travelled one last time throughout Crete to say his final farewells to the people. Most of those he had known in his early years had passed away, but the three sisters were still alive. He found them inside their whitewashed stone cottage. They no longer looked like the lovely young Graces. They were wrinkled with age and wore the black clothing of the widows of Crete.

Sir Arthur sat beside the first sister and watched her working at her spinning wheel. She was spinning wool into a string of yarn.

"Mister Evans," she asked, "have you found what you were looking for?"

"Not everything," he answered. "There are still so many mysteries left to solve. I don't know how to read the Minoans' ancient writing. I don't know their history or their language. I don't even know what they called themselves."

"What about the myths?" she asked him. "Don't they tell you anything?"

"They don't prove anything," he said. "They're just stories."

The second sister laughed softly to herself. She pulled the yarn out of the spinning wheel and let it unwind onto the floor. It made a tangled path almost too complicated to follow.

She said, "I remember a song that I learned from one of those stories."

She sang Sir Arthur the ancient song:

All living things must turn to dust
All metal things must turn to rust
All things must end someday.

"That song is very true," said Sir Arthur. "The Minoans had a great civilization, but there is very little left. Nothing lasts forever," he sighed.

"Watch this," said the third sister.

She cut the wool yarn from the spinning wheel. She rolled it into a ball, and she placed it inside a box.

"Now I have a riddle for *you*," she said. "What is not made of any thing at all, yet can outlast stone and bronze? It can keep its beauty longer than the finest palace. It can outlive kings and queens, heroes and monsters and even the Greek gods."

Sir Arthur thought for a long while. He did not want to give up, because he had always been very good at solving difficult questions. Finally, he shook his head. "I don't know," he said. "What is the answer?"

"A *story*," she said. "Stories are not made of stone or bronze or any thing at all. They are made of words, which are nothing more than sounds carried on the air. You might think they are so weak and momentary that they disappear like puffs of smoke. Yet, if the stories are good enough, like the myths of Crete, they will outlast everything and everyone."

The third sister gave Sir Arthur the box with the ball of wool yarn.

"This is our gift to you," she said. "You can use it to knit a sweater. Or you can use it as a long string to find your way through a labyrinth. Or you can leave it as it is to remind you of the amazing stories of this island."

Sir Arthur Evans accepted their gift and it became one of his greatest treasures.

GLOSSARY OF NAMES AND PLACES

ADRASTEIA. One of two beautiful female spirits of the ash trees. She was born from the blood of Uranos. She helped care for Zeus when he was a baby.

AEGEUS. King of Athens, father of Theseus. He was bewitched by Medea, who wanted to control Athens. The spell was broken by Theseus, whom Aegeus had fathered but never met, until Theseus came to claim his birthright. When Theseus sailed to Crete to stop the Minotaur, Aegeus told his crew to return bearing a white sail if he succeeded, and a black sail if he failed. Theseus succeeded but sailed back bearing a black sail. Some myths say he forgot, others say that a storm prevented him from changing the sail to white. Aegeus thought Theseus had been killed, so he leapt from a cliff into the sea, which is now named the Aegean Sea.

AMALTHEA. The Great Mother Goat. She was born from the blood of Uranos. She nursed Zeus in a mountain cave on Crete. Her horn became the Cornucopia, the Horn of Plenty that constantly provides wonderful foods. Some myths claim that Pan, the goat boy, was her son.

ANDROGEUS. Son of King Minos and Queen Pasiphae, Champion of the Athenian Games. He was killed trying to capture the Great White Bull on the plain of Marathon near Athens.

APOLLO. (Roman name—Sol) God of the sun, reason, prophecy, medicine, plague and music. Brother of Artemis, who was goddess of the Moon. Apollo drove the sun as a golden chariot across the sky, bringing each new day. He advised mortals through his oracle at Delphi. Daedalus built a temple to him in Italy.

ARGO. Jason and his crew of fifty-five heroes, called the *Argonauts*, sailed the *Argo* on their quest for the Golden Fleece. One myth says that it had been built by the gods as the first ship to sail the sea, and that Athena gave it the power of speech by placing in its bow a piece of an oak tree which was from a sacred oracle of Zeus.

ARIADNE. Daughter of King Minos and Queen Pasiphae. She gave Theseus a ball of thread to find his way out of the Labyrinth. She was unintentionally abandoned by Theseus on the island of Naxos, where she met the god Dionysus. They married and had four sons.

ATHENA. (Roman name—Minerva) Goddess of wisdom, war and the domestic arts such as weaving. She was born on Crete, emerging from the head of Zeus. Her symbols are the owl and the olive tree. Theseus sacrificed the Great White Bull at her temple in Athens.

ATHENS. The greatest city-state of ancient Greece. It was named for the goddess Athena. It gained freedom and power when the Minoan civilization collapsed. Minoan refugees brought important skills and knowledge to Athens. The myths of Theseus killing the Minotaur and of Theseus bringing Phaedra to Athens as his wife represent those historical events.

CERBERUS. The three-headed dog that guarded the entrance to the Underworld. Each head took turns keeping watch so no one could enter but the dead. Medea took the drool of Cerberus, which was called wolfsbane, to try to poison Theseus. Hercules later dragged the beast out of Hades to fulfil his twelfth and final task.

COCALUS. The King of Sicily who sheltered Daedalus from Minos. Daedalus built him a public steam bath, a fort and a palace. Daedalus later killed Minos, although another myth claims that it was King Cocalus' daughters, guided by Daedalus, who killed Minos, by boiling him alive in his bath.

CORONA BOREALIS. Also called the *Northern Crown*. A constellation that forms a semi-circle of seven stars in the Northern sky, near the Hercules constellation. It can be seen from February to September. Myths say that Dionysus gave it to Ariadne to wear at their wedding and then set its seven jewels into the sky.

CORNUCOPIA. Also called The Horn of Plenty. The Great Goat Mother, Amalthea, allowed Baby Zeus to break off her horn. It would miraculously stay full of delicious foods.

CRETE. The largest island in the Aegean Sea, south of Greece. It was the centre of the Minoan Civilization and is now part of modern Greece.

CRONOS. (Roman name—Saturn) A Titan. Youngest son of Uranos and Gaea, who were the first generation of gods. He took power from Uranos by wounding him in his bed, using a curved stone knife. He forced Rhea to be his wife, and she gave birth to six of the twelve Olympian gods: Zeus, Hades, Poseidon, Demeter, Hera and Hestia. After the Olympians defeated Cronos and his Titans, Cronos was banished to the Pit of Tartarus. Later, he repented. Zeus forgave him and sent him to rule the Isle of the Blessed beyond the known world.

CROWN OF LAURELS. The god Apollo's symbol of victory, which was awarded at the Great Games at Delphi. Apollo was often shown wearing a crown of laurels. However, his laurels actually came from a failure, not a success. Apollo had fallen in love with Daphne, a semi-divine maiden called a *nymph*. When he pursued her, she called to her father, a river god, for help, and she was transformed into a laurel tree. Apollo wore a crown of her leaves to remember his lost love.

THE CURETES. Also known as the Corybantes. The brothers of Rhea, Goddess of the Earth. Some myths say they were born from the rain, others say they were born from the earth. Still other myths describe them as forming from Rhea's fingers as she clutched the earth during childbirth. Their roars hid the wails of Baby Zeus so Cronos would not discover him. The priests of Rhea would shout and dance like the Curetes in a ritual reenactment of her suffering.

CYCLOPES. Three sons of Uranos and Gaea, who were defeated and imprisoned by Cronos. Each cyclops had a single eye in his forehead. Other cyclopes appear in Homer's Odyssey as giant cannibals, sons of Poseidon. One imprisons Odysseus in his cave, but Odysseus blinds him and escapes.

DAEDALUS. Said to be the inventor of the axe, wedge, level, sail, parasol, saw and winged flight. While constructing the roof for Athena's temple in Athens, he was angered by his nephew's boasting. He struck his nephew, who accidentally fell to his death. Other myths say Athena saved the boy by turning him into a bird. Guilt stricken, Daedalus fled to Crete and built the Labyrinth for Minos. He fled again because Minos accused him of helping Theseus navigate the maze and kill the Minotaur. Daedalus built wings for himself and his son, Icarus. Icarus flew too high. He fell to his death like Daedalus' nephew.

DEMETER. (Roman name—Ceres) Daughter of Cronos and Rhea. Mother of Plutus, god of wealth. Also mother of Persephone, goddess of the underworld and Spirit of the Spring. Demeter was goddess of the crops, who provided the power of growth and reproduction to all living things. When Hades kidnapped her daughter, Persephone, and took her to the Underworld, Demeter's grief stopped all growth on earth and caused the first winter.

DIA. Now called Naxos. Island in the Aegean Sea where Theseus was forced to leave Ariadne. Dionysus rescued and married her.

DIONYSUS. (Roman name—Bacchus) Youngest of the Olympians. God of wine, wild music and ecstatic celebrations. He introduced grapes and wine from the Far East, which made him both the God of Madness and the God of Joy. He married Ariadne, settled down somewhat, and had four children.

ELYSIUM FIELDS. Home of the Blessed in the Underworld; Paradise. It was seen as a reward for the souls of great heroes. The Champs-Elysées, a grand street in Paris, is named after it.

EUROPA. Daughter of Agenor. Princess of Phoenicia, a land on the eastern Mediterranean near present-day Syria. The Phoenicians were merchant sailors who created oared ships that sailed great distances. They also invented the alphabet to record business transactions. Princess Europa was kidnapped and taken to Crete by Zeus, who took the shape of a bull. Some myths claim that they married and had three sons, and that the rulers of Crete were her semi-divine descendants.

EVANS, SIR ARTHUR. British archaeologist (1851-1941). He began exploring sites on Crete in 1896. In 1900, he discovered the Palace of Minos during an archaeological dig at Knossos. He restored and rebuilt important parts of the palace and brought to light the Minoan civilization. He was knighted for his work by the King of England in 1911. Sir Arthur continued working at Knossos until he returned to England in 1935, at the age of eighty-four.

FURIES. Three sisters—Alecto (Unrest), Megaera (Jealousy), and Tisiphone (Vengeance)—born from the blood of Uranos when he was wounded by his son, Cronos. The Furies haunted those who dared to harm their own parents.

GREAT GAMES. Many areas of Greece had athletic games, which were combined with religious festivals. The games at Delphi were dedicated to Apollo, and a crown of laurels was top prize. The games in Olympia were dedicated to Zeus, and the winners were awarded a wreath of olive leaves from Zeus's holy tree. Little is known about the early games at Athens. Later, about 800 BC, the Olympic Games were founded, which included athletes from all over Greece. There were seven days of track and field competitions, with no team events. During the games a Holy Truce was declared, temporarily halting any wars that were occurring between the city-states.

GREAT WHITE BULL. Also called the Cretan Bull and the Bull of Marathon. Sent to King Minos by the god Poseidon. When Minos refused to return it by sacrificing it to Poseidon, the god made the bull go mad. It ravaged Crete and caused Queen Pasiphae to give birth to the Minotaur. Hercules captured it to fulfil one of his twelve tasks. It escaped and killed Androgeus when he tried to recapture it. Theseus caught the bull and sacrificed it to the goddess Athena.

GRYPHON. Also spelled *griffin*. Mythical beast with the head of a wingless eagle and the body of a lion. The eagle symbolizes spiritual power, while the lion symbolizes physical power. The wall paintings of gryphons

99

at the palace at Knossos were created by a method called fresco, which used earth hues pressed onto fresh wet plaster walls.

HADES. (Roman name—Pluto) The Underworld, as well as the name of the god of the Underworld. Hades was an Olympian, son of Cronos and Rhea. He kidnapped Persephone, spirit of the spring, and forced her to live with him in the Underworld for part of each year. Her absence caused winter in the world above.

HEPHAESTUS. (Roman name—Vulcan, as in volcano) God of fire. Son of Zeus and Hera, he was crippled when Hera tossed him out of the sky at birth because of his weakness and ugliness. Ironically, he became a creator of powerful weapons and beautiful jewellery. He used volcanic fires to forge metal for other creations, such as Talus, the Bronze Giant. Hephaestus was worshipped by blacksmiths and craftsmen.

HERA. (Roman name—Juno) Goddess of the Earth, women and childbirth; wife of Zeus and queen of the gods; daughter of Cronos and Rhea.

HERCULES. (Roman name for the Greek hero Heracles) Son of Zeus and Alcmene. He was a hero of great strength and passion but little wisdom. He killed his wife and children in a fit of madness caused by the goddess Hera. The Delphic Oracle told him he could cleanse his guilt if he performed twelve tasks for King Eurystheus. One task was to bring Eurystheus the Great White Bull of Crete. Hercules accomplished all the tasks. He also sailed on the *Argo* with Jason in the quest for the Golden Fleece. He abandoned the quest to search for a young Argonaut who had gone missing, so he was not with the Argonauts when they were attacked by Talus, the Bronze Giant.

100

HERMES. (Roman name—Mercury) Son of Zeus and Maia; a master of tricks and clever words; messenger of Zeus; god of merchants, thieves, travel and boundaries. He delivered both true and false dreams from the two gates of Hades and guided souls to the Underworld, such as the soul of Androgeus after the Great White Bull killed him.

HESTIA. (Roman name—Vesta) Daughter of Cronos and Rhea; goddess of the hearth and home; one of the gods swallowed by Cronos. She forbade gossip because it harmed families and communities. Therefore, no stories were told about her.

HUNDRED-HANDED ONES. Monstrous offspring of Uranos. Cronos cast them into the Pit of Tartarus, but Zeus freed them to fight against Cronos and the Titans, whom they pelted with countless rocks. They returned to Tartarus to guard the defeated Titans.

ICARIA. An island in the Aegean named after Icarus, who was buried there by his father, Daedalus.

ICARUS. The son of Daedalus. His reckless pride—which the Greeks called *hubris*—caused him to fly too high and then plunge into the sea. Myths claim the sun melted the wax that was holding together his feathers. That is not exactly true, because the air is cooler at higher levels. However, as modern hang-gliders have discovered, when the sun shines on the earth or sea on a hot day, it produces rising columns of hot air that can lift a hang-glider to great heights. The heat from a column of hot air can also melt wax.

Io. One of two beautiful female spirits of the ash trees. She was born from the blood of Uranos. She helped care for Zeus when he was a baby.

JASON. Leader of the Argonauts, who led the quest for the Golden Fleece. He sailed his ship, the *Argo*, to Colchis, a land along the Black Sea. He accepted help from Medea, a sorceress, but he regretted it when her actions became increasingly evil. He won the Fleece but could not rid himself of Medea for many years. By then, his pride and reputation as a hero were destroyed.

KALLISTE. Later called Thera and then Santorini. A Minoan volcanic island between Crete and Greece. Its population was highly advanced in art and science, with indoor toilets, showers, and hot and cold running water. The island was partially destroyed by a volcano about 1,450 BC (the same time period the Hebrews left Egypt). The eruption was the fourth largest in the last 100,000 years, equal to the explosion of 150 hydrogen bombs, and it could have been heard 3,000 kilometers or 2,000 miles away. It caused a tidal wave that was sixty stories high when it struck Turkey and parts of Greece. The eruption and the following tidal wave and ash cloud devastated Crete. Further earthquakes, eruptions and deep layers of ash made it impossible for the Minoans to rebuild. Recent evidence suggests Kalliste was Plato's Atlantis.

KNOSSOS. The capital of the Minoan civilization of Crete. The palace at Knossos was the size of England's Buckingham Palace, with five floors and a thousand rooms. It was destroyed by earthquakes and buried in volcanic ash around 1,450 BC. Fifty years later, more earthquakes ended all attempts to rebuild it.

LABYRINTH. A maze that was built beneath the Palace of Knossos by Daedalus to imprison the Minotaur. Ariadne gave Theseus a ball of string to navigate the maze and kill the Minotaur. However, archaeologists have not found any actual proof of a labyrinth in the palace. Mazes did exist in the region, even in prehistoric times, and the five storey palace with its thousand rooms would have seemed like a maze, which might have led to the myth of a labyrinth. The word labyrinth comes from the name of the double-headed axe of Minoan warriors and priests. Images of the axe were found on the walls of the palace. The idea of a bull or bull-man in the labyrinth is a natural addition to the myth. Bulls were a sacred animal on Crete and were probably kept in the palace area. Their images were everywhere, and their horns adorned many roofs. The palace had acrobatic games and rituals with sacred bulls. There is also evidence that a bull was being sacrificed even while earthquakes and volcanic eruptions were destroying the palace.

MARATHON. A plain east of Athens, near the sea, where Androgeus was killed trying to capture the Great White Bull. Later, in 490 BC, 11,000 Greeks defeated a much larger invading army of Persians, killing 6,000 while losing only 192 men. Legends claim that the armed spirit of Theseus led the Greek forces. A Greek soldier ran the 26 miles to Athens to alert the city. Just as he reached his goal, he collapsed and died. The present day long distance race is called a *marathon* in memory of that soldier's heroic run.

MEDEA. A sorceress of the black arts. Daughter of Aeetes, sorcerer king of Colchis. She helped Jason win the Golden Fleece, and defeated Talus, the Bronze Giant. When Jason broke free from her evil control, she fled to Athens, where she bewitched King Aegeus so she could marry him and rule Athens. However, Medea failed to stop Theseus, Aegeus's long lost son, from claiming his birthright. She fled back to Colchis on a chariot pulled by dragons.

MINOS. Son of Europa and Zeus; first king and a great lawmaker of the Minoans. All kings afterwards were called Minos. When Minos died, he became one of the three judges of the Underworld. The laws of Minos

101

lasted for the 1,800-year span of Crete's civilization and were later passed on to the Greeks. The last King Minos offended Zeus. This led to the destruction of the Bronze Giant, which guarded Crete. King Minos then offended Poseidon, which resulted in the birth of the Minotaur. Minos changed Crete from a merchant power to a military power with control over parts of Greece. He died in Sicily while pursuing Daedalus. His daughter, Queen Phaedra, inherited the kingdom, which was soon destroyed by earthquakes and volcanic blasts.

MINOTAUR. The monster with the body of a man and head of a bull. The Minotaur was kept in the Labyrinth and killed by Theseus. There are conflicting myths about his parentage. One historian claims the Minotaur was a mythic representation of a Minoan general named Tauros (meaning *bull*), who was defeated by Theseus in personal combat. Bulls were a symbol of the Minoans, whose power was based on the sea and who revered bulls as sacred creatures of Poseidon, god of the sea.

MOUNT DICTE. Now called Mt. Lasithi. Where Zeus was sheltered in a cave as a baby. The cave remained a place of worship, where the Minoan kings and queens went for inspiration and to offer sacrifices.

MOUNT IDA. Now called Mt. Aegeum. On Crete where Zeus lived as a child.

MOUNT OLYMPUS. Home of the third generation of gods, the Olympians.

MOUNT OTHRYS OF CRONOS. Fortress of Cronos and his Titans.

OLIVE BRANCH OF ATHENA. Athena was the patron goddess of Athens. The olive tree, which was sacred to her worship, was highly important to Athens because it provided both food and oil for lamps. It was a symbol of Athena's blessings and is now a universal symbol of peace. Ironically, Athena was not only the goddess of wisdom, but also the goddess of war.

ORACLE OF DELPHI. An oracle tells a prophecy of the future. Apollo, above all other gods, had the power to prophesy. He answered questions for many centuries, through a priestess at his temple in Delphi. Historians describe the priestess sitting in Apollo's temple, suspended from a tripod over a crack in the earth. Fumes rising from the earth put her into a trance, and it was believed that the god would then speak using her voice. The answers could be difficult to understand. For example, King Croesus asked if he should attack Persia. The oracle said that if he attacked Persia, he would destroy a mighty empire. He attacked, but he was defeated and captured. He then realised that the mighty empire he destroyed was his own.

PAN. Part human, part goat. Some myths say he was the son of Hermes. He was Zeus's companion on Mount Ida and fought the Titans with his war cry, which caused panic (derived from the word *Pan*). He resembled the satyrs of Dionysus in his goatish appearance, love of music and physical desires.

PASIPHAE. Wife of Minos; mother of Androgeus, Phaedra, Ariadne and the Minotaur.

PHAEDRA. Daughter of Minos and Pasiphae, she was the last Queen of Crete. She married Theseus, became Queen of Athens and passed on the knowledge of her civilization.

PIT OF TARTARUS. The deepest, darkest part of Hades (the Underworld), where the Titans were imprisoned along with others who offended the gods. One human prisoner was Sisyphus, who forever had to struggle to roll a boulder to the top of a hill, only to watch it fall back just before he reached his goal. Another was

Tantalus, who was chained centimeters away from tantalizing food, as he stood chin deep in water that would drain away if he tried to drink it.

POSEIDON. (Roman name—Neptune) Also called Father Horse, Lord of Bulls, Tamer of Horses, Girder of the World and Earth Shaker. The son of Cronos and Rhea, he was the God of the Sea. His weapon was the trident, a three pronged fishing spear. He built his underwater palace in the Aegean Sea. He created the horse, bull and dolphin as his sacred creatures. Ancient people believed that earthquakes were caused by tidal waves sent by Poseidon.

RHEA. Daughter of Uranos and Gaea; wife of Cronos. She was the Earth Mother Goddess like her mother, Gaea, before her, and her daughter Hera after her. In earlier times, people believed she was the earth itself. At first, the Minoans of Crete worshipped only the Earth Mother. Afterwards, as they accepted the idea of Zeus the Sky Father, they claimed that he was brought to Crete by the Earth Mother and born in a mountain cave.

TALUS. The last of a race of bronze giants, though some myths say he was created by Hephaestus, god of fire. Zeus sent Talus to protect Crete, circling the island three times a day so Crete did not have to fortify its cities. Medea defeated Talus by draining his life liquid, called *ichor*, from his Achilles heel. Another myth said she cursed him as he picked up a rock to strike the *Argo*. This caused him to graze himself with the rock, allowing his ichor to drain away.

THESEUS. Son of Aegeus and Aethra. He conquered the bandit kings between Troezen and Athens. He caught the Great White Bull, then defeated Medea and the Minotaur. Some say that Theseus' fight with the Minotaur is a mythic way to describe the Greek revolt against the Minoans. Theseus also defeated the Amazons and later the Centaurs, an army of creatures that were half man, half horse. When he tried to rescue Persephone from Hades, he was trapped in the Chair of Forgetfulness but was saved by Hercules. He brought Phaedra from Crete and married her, which may represent the transfer of power and knowledge from the dying Minoan civilization to the rising Greek civilization.

TITANS. The giant children of Uranos and Gaea, who were defeated by the Olympians. Atlas, who led the Titans, was forced to hold up the sky until he was transformed into the Atlas Mountains. The Titan Prometheus (which means *foresight*) took the side of the Olympians. He later created humans, but Zeus punished him for giving them the power of fire.

ZEUS. (Roman name—Jupiter) God of the Sky. Ruler of the Gods. Son of Cronos and Rhea. He took on many forms: rain, a bull, a shower of gold, a swan, a flame. One legend says that he married Europa and the kings of Crete were his semi-divine children. He had countless children with both gods and humans. The Minoans worshipped Zeus at his birth cave on Mount Dicte, where he blessed and advised Crete's rulers.

AFTERWORD

The myths of the Minoan civilization reveal how the ancient Greeks remembered their distant past. This past pre-dated the introduction of the alphabet; it survived in the songs of the bards, professional tellers of tales, the living archives of their people. Imagination enlivened these stories with gods, goddesses, monsters, heroes, villains, heroines and witches. For the Greeks, these tales were a rich cultural heritage. From this source later artists, poets and dramatists drew the plots and characters through which they examined contemporary human concerns. In the Fifth Century BC, the historian Thucydides credited Minos and his fleet with suppressing piracy in the Aegean Sea. Yet to the ancient Greeks, Crete was also a land of wonders and adventure. ꙮ The excavations of modern archaeologists have revealed much about the physical background of the Bronze Age, the power of Crete, the beauty of its art and the expertise of its craftsmen. Every year brings new discoveries, but the interpretation of this evidence, the precise dating of events, their causes, their relationship to each other and to the ancient myths, remain open to scholarly debate. Yet the power of myth to stimulate the interest of artists, writers and readers will always remain, as new generations see, hear, and come to love these stories about the island of the Minotaur, imaginatively interwoven by modern storytellers like Sheldon Oberman. ꙮ

— Robert Gold, Associate Professor of Classics (retired), University of Winnipeg